TRUST

No
One

BY MR. GRAM

outskirts
press

Outskirts Press, Inc.
http://www.outskirtspress.com

ISBN: 978-1-9772-0193-5

Outskirts Press and the "OP" logo are trademarks belonging to Outskirts Press, Inc.

PRINTED IN THE UNITED STATES OF AMERICA

*The Characters and turn of events in this novel
are all fictional.*

0

I never chose to write an urban story; to glorify the lifestyle in our hoods. I write these kinds of stories only because I have lived it and I advise you not to! But we need to understand there will never be a positive outcome from such negativity. In an environment where all praise the dollar, you tend to lose loyalty to those around you. Life no longer is respected, and a friend becomes a dollar in your pocket.

Me, personally, I was subjected to the game and became a MONSTER, someone not to trust. It's not because I'm a disloyal person or not trustworthy. It's because I've learned to live by one rule to guarantee my survival in the jungle and that is to TRUST NO ONE!

I've seen it one to many times where the closest one to you did the pulling of the trigger. They say that only the wise man could learn from others mistake. So, put me in that category cause I would not let anyone play me close enough to stab me in the back or better yet harm me.

So, I warn you all to keep your eyes open and your ears to the ground because it's really a jungle out there. A jungle that has no remorse, no loyalty, no friends, and no pity. Me, I can consider myself lucky for surviving the hell that I've lived, through prison and the concrete jungle! But you all, you all can be smarter than me and consider not being in this chaotic underworld for a second!

CHAPTER 1

The temperature was twelve degrees but with the wind chill it felt more like zero. The streets were deserted due to the Super Bowl game except for those enslaved to narcotics. The only sounds that were heard on the block came from the people viewing the champions to be, Patriots playing against the Los Angeles Rams. It was a battle between a young core of players verses on of the greatest quarter backs that played the game.

Omar was nervously parked in a Dodge Charger two buildings down from where the rest were. They were on 147th street between Broadway and Amsterdam. Omar could not believe he was there with the rest, but if anything, he only questioned Chucks sanity. Omar was a small man and not much of a livewire, but his driving skills were Chuck's reason for giving him the getaway job. The other reason is that Omar and X are childhood friends and they could not find another person that they could trust for such a job.

Omar was thinking to himself, how could Chuck pick today out of all days to hit this spot, for crying out loud this was Broadway. But like they say, there is not much of a difference between a genius and a lunatic. The only thing Omar prayed for was that Chuck was no lunatic. Omar's task was to sit patiently in the car and alert the team whenever he spotted the carrier walking towards the building. Then, get them home once they get what they came for. Omar had butterflies in his stomach, even though his driving skills are superb, he never used them for a stickup. But thinking on what was in it for him, helped him stay put through these nerve wrecking moments. But it still did not prevent him from praying to God that everything went well.

Chuck, Bump-off, and X were in the drug spot with the connect. It was a run-down spot with holes on the walls and a ceiling that looked like it may come down at any second, but the apartment served its purpose. They had a futon, a television, an X-box 360 sitting on crates and a triple beam scale sitting on a desk. While Bump sat on the futon with Jose playing a game on the X-box, X ran his mouth to Sosa, sniffing line after line of coke keeping him at bay.

Chuck stayed calm using his 20/20 vision to keep track of the gun man that Sosa kept in the bedroom just in case anyone tried what they are about to attempt. They did a horrible job at it because they were to obvious. To be honest, a blind man could clearly see that someone was behind the door by the silhouette seen under the door. The entire building was rowdy with the cheering and thumping from those watching the game in the other apartments. That was Chuck's reason for trying Sosa out today of all days. What better time than a time that damn near the entire city was under the influence of drugs or alcohol partying and watching the game? Chuck observed the room and was amazed at how Sosa could be so connected but so reckless at the same time. He spent his entire bid up north talking about all the money he made in the streets and how he was going to do this and that when he got out. He let everyone know his business and today is the day that all that bragging is going to cost him dearly. If there is one thing Chuck will not do, is leave someone alive when he has done dirt to them.

It has happened way too often where the past comes and bites you in the ass, just because you made the mistake of letting someone live. Chuck always found humor in X's way of being. Being his baby cousin is what allowed him to look past X's ways. It wasn't until Chuck was in the prison system that X started to get his hands dirty in the streets and there is not too much you can tell anyone when you are behind those walls.

But now that Chuck is out, he clearly sees what the streets made of him. Now X, he's a complete terror with balls of steel! His lifestyle consists of hustling, women and partying hard. At six foot three and 220 pounds, it is hard to tell that he pulls all-nighters. Especially with his Clark Kent look, you would think he's more of a college student. That's something that Chuck cannot stand about his little cousin, when he starts to party, he could sniff coke for days. And at times it can distract him from his work ethics. Now Bump, he was the total opposite of X, sometimes it even surprised Chuck how X and Bump linked up. Bump was one hundred and ten percent gangster.

A money getter that let his gun do the talking with no other bad habits except for liquor. At times Bump reminded Chuck of O-Dog from Menace to Society. Young and black, with the only difference being he was too smart to not give a fuck. Bump was short and stocky with the resemblance of a N.F.L. running back.

When Chuck's phone rang, he knew that the mule was on his way to the crib. The only person with his phone number was Omar but he played it off. He spoke out loud so that everyone in the apartment heard him, especially his team. "This fucking bitch, I'm tired of her ass calling me all day!"

That's his way of telling X and Bump the time to put that work in was almost here. It was also a way of relaxing Sosa a little because having females on their asses giving them a hard time, is something they could all relate too. Chuck knew that his relationship with Sosa was going to change the moment his little brother got in the apartment. That's what he was looking forward to the most. Chuck made eye contact with Bump and could see the hunger in his eyes. He was accustomed to a lifestyle that was distracted by his ex-comrade, Stone. Now he was willing to do anything to get his status and money up to where it was before. He had been through too much to be broke this deep in the game. So, if it meant putting that work in to come up, you best to believe it was going to happen. For he was married to the game and didn't want a divorce no time soon.

Jacob was so happy that Chuck came to purchase again. He was the only customer that earns him a few grand at a time. This time around would be the first time that would earn him five G's in one lump sum. So, if it was one thing for sure, his love for Chuck was growing every time he saw him. Jacob came from the

Dominican Republic and at the age of nineteen; he had already purchased a house for his mother back home in D.R. The game treated him well and in return he took care of those that were back in his country. Looking no more than fourteen years.

This delivery right here was what was going to fund the trip.

Sosa is the one that demanded that he dress like a kid and stay under the radar. His older brother showed him the game and dropped many jewels about it also. But if there is one, he should have stressed a lot more it was not to give your trust up so easily. He walked by two officers on foot, but he knew that by his appearance he would not be harassed. If only he would've known what was to come, he probably would've cried out for help. There's only one thing promised the moment you are born and that's death. The sad thing is, we will never know when it comes knocking at our doors calling our name.

Jacob was getting exhausted carrying the ten bricks, but he had no time to rest. He just kept thinking "there's money to be made". He walked in long strides focused, trying to get to his destination. He walked right by Omar without even looking in his direction. DEADLY MISTAKE! He was oblivious to his surroundings, all he worried about was making his drop off and getting his cut. He ran up the stairs and felt a load off his shoulders the moment he knocked on the door.

There was a loud knock on the door. Jose paused the game being played between him and Bump; and hopped up to answer the door. Bump got up to follow. With any other customer, Sosa might have felt uncomfortable to the point where his guards would of went up. But since he's known Chuck for so long his spider senses never went off.

Jose opened the door for Jacob and let him in quickly. "What's up Bump?" He greeted him as he walked passed him and Jose. In a rush to finish their transactions so that he could get his paper and go about his business.

Jose went to lock the door, but Bump insisted on locking it for him.

"Thanks, Bump, for being such a gentleman." Jose kidded.

"No problem my friend." Bump replied knowing what's to come.

Bump locked, then turned from the door and in turning around he reached into his waist to pull out his two twin .357 Magnums. He did not waste a second to do his duty, he aimed one gun at Jose and the other at Jacob. Jose saw what was about to happen. But before he could say anything his vision went blank. Bump put rounds into Jose and Jacobs head simultaneously.

X then quick drew his arms and let off three shots. BOOM, BOOM, BOOM! Hitting Sosa in the face with all 3 shots, he was dead before he ever hit the floor. Chuck at the same time fired his entire clip of his desert eagle, murdering Sosa's goon without ever looking at his face.

The stickup Gods must have been on their side. It was only a second before Jacob walked into the apartment that Tom Brady threw a touchdown pass to Gronkowski, which had the entire building in an uproar of cheers and cries. Chuck grabbed the duffel bag looked through the peep hole, unlocked the door, then strolled out. The rest of the crew began to follow when Chuck suddenly stopped in his tracks to remind Bump to grab the Xbox remote, he was using. Chuck knew from experience that a little slip up like that could bring a lot of consequences later. Shit the entire penal system is filled with criminals that made small mistakes just like that. And Chuck was not trying to be one of them.

Omar's phone rang, it was Chuck, the call he had been waiting for. He took his foot off the break and pulled around to the front of the building right on time as the clique walked out of the entrance. Once they jumped in the whip, Omar accelerated his speed but not in a way to attract attention.

Everyone was quiet on the way home. Chuck was just happy he had a team of brave hearts. Otherwise, they would still just be talking about coming up from their losses, contemplating moves without taking affirmative action on them.

X broke the silence by calling Chuck's phone, while getting on the I-95 north from the west side highway. Chuck looked at his phone and instantly threw it out the window for it already served its purpose.

"We did it comrades, we did it." He did not say much for the rest of the ride. He just sat quietly as his thoughts went to bigger and better things.

CHAPTER 2

ONE YEAR EARLIER

It was New Year's Eve and the team celebrated the upcoming year in an after-hour spot somewhere in the Bronx. It was a place where hustlers came to show off their financial status. It's a hole in the wall to many, except for a few made men that really knew about it. But the difference tonight was that the only people invited to celebrate this ball drop was those personally invited by Stone. If you were not part of the family, you had to celebrate somewhere else. Stone put in a lot of work in the last few months. From not having much to a guy that was able to buy out the spot for the night. You could tell that he was feeling accomplished coming into the new year.

He dressed as always, in his Goon attire; a cone

head black champion hood, a dark pair of Levi jeans, all black chukkas, Cartier frames, a trademark jacket for Bronx Earners, a Marc Buchanan butter soft, and Cuban chain with the Jesus piece, that was easily the most expensive item he owned. Now at six feet two inches, two hundred pounds he had the body of a grown man with a baby face. But by the way he moved, others knew he was not one to be taken lightly. There is not many that can truly fuck with him or outshine him in the game he is playing in these streets.

Being rugged, pretty, and silent is what attracted many to him. He is a total gentleman; someone you can rely on. But in return he was a savage, a man you could not cross. He is always with his two Riders that look like God's own personal gifts to earth. The females that always stand to his side are Cindy, a gorgeous Puerto Rican and African American woman, with a face of pure innocence. At 5"2', 125 pounds, no one would ever see her coming.

She was beautiful an absolute doll but in return she was deadly to those that oppose the movement. She has been riding with Stone, since the day he first step foot into the game.

Now Chinas physique is totally different from Cindy. Instead of being short and thick she was tall and slim with the extra weight in all the right places. When asked of her nationality her answer was always the same, Exotic! She always stays put by Stones side looking fabulous. It was never planned, they just understood that they had to play their positions to a tee. Stone didn't just have the sexiest females in the hood. He had them doing whatever he wanted them to do with them enjoying every moment of it.

Stone was enjoying the high from the Molly that China gave him. Through his peripheral he saw his team on the dance floor having a ball. Bump couldn't dance for shit but who was going to tell him anything. This was the first New Years that he really balled out enjoying himself. Bump grew up in Forest projects a low-income family housing where seventy percent of the people lived off public assistance and what they could hustle up in the streets. As a child Bump lived in a very hectic household mainly because his mama was a crack addict and his dad was a dealer, that kept taking losses due to his mother's habits. So how hard was it too realize, the reason they fought from sunup to sundown was due to drugs and them mysteriously disappearing. They had loved each other till mom chose to love drugs more than she loved herself and her family. It got to the point where dad wanted no part of her and the only reason, he stayed at the house was because he wanted to raise his son and give him all life had to offer, including a mother.

One day Stone asked Bump a simple question and that was one of the reason their bond grew so strong overnight. "Why did you move uptown with your Grandma just to live in this raggedy ass hood?" This was a time when they used to chip in for weed and share small talk. I guess they were trying to figure each other out.

Bump had his back turned to Stone and was quiet for about a minute before turning around with a face full of tears. "My dad couldn't take the stealing from my mom and killed her with his hands. Right in front of me, Stone, he choked her out. Do you know what I did to stop my father from killing my mom?"

"What you do Bump?"

"Nothing, I did nothing to try to stop it Stone! I just stood there and begged my father to stop but I never attempted to do anything. I was only ten, but I knew I should have tried to do something to stop it. If I could have just stopped it somehow, instead of freezing like a bitch when my mom needed me most. She would still be here, and pops wouldn't be rotting away behind the wall. She was an addict and all but that was my mother. She gave me life and I wish I could have shared more moments with her in my lifetime." Stone could still remember that day like it was yesterday.

Stone could easily relate to the poverty, the pain and the struggle that life usually brings to the poor. His family came from Puerto Rico without a plan, an education, or money to support their family. So, for Stone, hard times and hunger pains were as regular as taking a piss in the project elevators. But that was then, and now it's a different time. It's a time that they can do almost whatever the fuck they want to do. Shit, Stone is getting to the point where he put money on the scale to count it because it has become a pain in the ass to count by hand.

He still remembered the expression on his mom's face when he bought her, her own home. That was just last week and to get that look on his mom's face again, he'll kill another man, or two, without it tampering with his conscious.

"FIVE! FOUR! THREE!" Cindy tapped Stone on the arm to get him out of his thoughts. "Happy New Year!" Everyone had their own bottle to pop to bring in the New Year. Bump, B-blast, and the rest of the squad sat around Stone with a bunch of females. Stone gave eye contact to his comrades lifting his bottle, then gave a toast for the New Year. "To us my brothers. Just know, united we stand, separated we fall."

"Say it again Stone!" Pretty boy yelled so that Stone could hear him from across the table.

"To us!" Stone yelled and in return the crowd cheered. "Again!"

"To us!" Stone shouted above the crowd. "I want to tell you all I appreciate you spending the night with us. I swear if we didn't move as a team, we would not have made it this far." Stone got up and asked Bump and Blast to walk with him.

"I just want to let you know that this is going to be our year..." Stone started as they walked away from the crowd.

"Shit this is our year already Stone. We came up a long way already." Blast said.

"No, we came up this year bro, but this is the year we going to fly high! Believe me, you'll see what I am talking about."

"No doubt Blood, I got faith in you" Bump said. But deep down inside he envied Stone. He knew it was Stone that was getting all the respect, all the power, and all the recognition for what they were doing as a team. He thought to himself "I need more, Shit I could do it too. But there was one thing if I do it, that is the moment Stone must be out the picture for good. Then it would be the rest of the team I have to worry about. It won't be a good move to try to take Stone out in the open. If there is one thing the team does not tolerate is disloyalty. He's made examples already of what happens to the disloyal."

At that moment he swore that the moment he caught Stone even blinking, the attempt on his life would be taken without the rest knowing. Cause the importance of it all is that the rest do not find out when it's done. Only because the benefits will not be worth the headache and the wrath that comes with Stone's death.

As they spoke Stone got a funny vibe from Bump. He decided to tell him to be patient that the money is coming real soon, it was only to throw him off. It was the way that Bump kept his eyes on him all the time with so many face expressions showing him a negative vibe. "Yo Bump, I got a few spots out here for you where you can get your own money, I mean if you're interested, but there's one thing Bump that I'm going to go ahead and put out there." They stopped walking and Stone looked deep into Bumps eyes giving him the most serious look he can make, it was one of a maniac, a straight killer!

Bump could see that Stone was going to keep it real as far as not biting his tongue and saying what he feels as always. "What's that Stone?"

"Don't cross me dog... I mean it" He spoke with a snarl to his voice. "My love for you has grown over time, to even think of doing to you what I had to do to Benny hurts me."

"What are you talking about Stone, you bugging

out man." Bump never shared his thoughts with any-one, so it was impossible for Stone to know what he was thinking. It was as if he read his mind and that alone put Bump on edge. He played it cool, ton-ing down his body language. "I will never cross you Stone, I swear you have been nothing but good to me. I would be a fool to mess up this relationship, when you only have been a brother to me."

"I just hope you don't try anything stupid my G. I play to win expecting the unexpected at all times."

Bump was ready to lose it, but thanks to China their conversation was interrupted. She pulled Stone away putting that topic on pause for the moment. "I do not care how busy you are Stone. We are going to dance at least one song."

"Come on China you already know that I don't dance. I'm always too busy keeping my eyes on every-thing that's going on around me." He decided to let Bump off the leash for now because he has been an asset to the cause so far.

"Aww come on just this one-time babes?" she curled her lips and tried to give her best impression of a sad puppy.

"Don't give me that look you already know I'm not dancing. We can slide off to the cut and have our personal time and you can do what you do bet-ter than dancing if you got the feeling for it love."

But me on that dance floor, that's a no-no. "Even better!" She said with a smile pulling him by the arm leading the way to a secluded area.

As they walked over to an off-limits area and started to get a little freaky a loud crash came from the entrance of the club which got his attention.

"What the fuck was that?", Stone asked looking around, Stone then ran towards the entrance of the lounge. What he saw next really got under his skin for he disliked this man so much. X and his little team done did one of the bouncers dirty, beating him bloody. Blast had X in a bear hug trying to get him out the exit while the rest of the crew did the same with the others.

"Fuck that nigga Stone! X yelled loudly as he was getting man handled by Blast, I don't give a fuck about him, or that this is his party!"

"Yo Blast let him go!" Stone ordered.

"Yeah Blast! Get your hands off me before you regret it." Blast only let him go because Stone ordered him to do so. Otherwise he would have been outside by now on his back.

"For as long as I have known you, we've had nothing but bad encounters. I don't know X it seems to me that you trying to give me a reason to do something terrible to you. The funny shit is that you don't seem to understand that I am not trying to waste my time with small fries like you. Since there is no gain for me to eliminate you from my picture, I allow you to remain standing here right now. So, I suggest you try to keep me from finding that reason."

X couldn't believe Stones cockiness, "How you know it wouldn't be the other way around? I mean you bleed just like me Stone so any one of us can get it. Because you are not smart enough to pull it off! Now I'm giving you the opportunity to walk out of this door on your own free will. If not…"

"If not," what X yelled getting all amped up of the way Stone spoke to him.

Stone laughed a little then simply told him, "You get put out!" Stone motioned to Blast with a nod of the head and within seconds X and his little entourage were out in the cold on the concrete floor face down. X was about to retaliate but his mind changed the moment he saw the two patrol cars coming up the block. "Every dog has his day and Stone and it's going to be me who brings it to you." He thought to himself.

Biggie wasn't lying when he said more money more problems, Stone thought. Stone knew the game he chose to play so to play it right, his trust would be something he would give to no one. How can I trust a man when I can't trust myself to do what's right for me? That was one of the many things he learned from his pops that stuck with him out in these streets.

Stone decided to call it the night because tomorrow was sure to be a tiring day for him with his traveling. He has a flight to Florida to meet up with some very influential people in the drug trade.

"I had enough for the night I'm out of here." Stone got up and walked off with his two ladies' following him. Outside sat Stones personal driver that he used every time he went out to get his drink on. House was loyal to Stone because it was Stone's money that got him his car. The true reason he did this for him was so that he can stay in school and stay on the right path. He was never around when it was time to make money or get their hands dirty. As intimidating as he looked house was just a good dude staying out of trouble in this negative world. He was one out of a hundred that let the rest know we do not have to be a product of our environment just because we come up in it.

As House pulled off, he seen something that he hoped Stone did not see, X entering the establishment. The two had a rep and bad blood for one another so when the two collide for sure there will be a casualty or two.

Stone seen X go in but there are plenty more important things to do right now. Someday everyone must pay the piper, lucky for X there's not that many hours in this day. "Don't worry X I got something coming for you, it's only a matter of time my G, just a matter of time." Then just as quick his thoughts moved on to the trip ahead of him the following day. "I hope they about their business for real cause if they are then I will be on the map for sure getting all the money out here!"

CHAPTER 3

This was Stones first time on a plane, and he swore he'd never do it again. For one, he feared heights way before the flight but when the plane dealt with turbulence 20,000 feet in the air, he most definitely lost his cool up there, terrified like never. "Hell, no I will never get on this shit again, please get me out of this lord", those were the exact words that ran through his head as the plane had an earthquake way up in the sky. Once in Miami airport the second he got to the pickup area a small man approached Stone.

"With all due respect, are you Mr. Stone?", I'm here on behalf of Manalo".

"Yes, I am, and you are?" putting his hand out so the undersized man could shake his hand, still clueless of who this man is.

"My name is Santos", grabbing Stones hand squeezing hard enough to indirectly let him know to take him seriously. And not to underestimate him cause he's a pint size man. "Well Mr. Stone let me help you with your bag. I hope you have a pleasant stay while you in Miami. Now please come with me, we got to take a cab so that we can go to where our cars are parked".

"No problem Santos", Stone tailed Santos, got into a cab and said nothing for the five-minute drive. It was all good for Stone because the truth of the matter is, he was enjoying the view, never in his lifetime did he leave the hood. They drove into an indoor parking lot that stored all the top-notch vehicles from Lambo's to Ferrari's making the place look like a car show more than anything.

"Well Mr. Stone, this is going to be your car as long as you are Manalo's guess." Pointing at the 600 Benz that had the keys in the ignition. "Use the navigation system to guide you where you are going to meet with the Boss. The location of where you will meet him at is logged in on the GPS already."

Stone got confused for a second, he did not know he was going to travel on his own. "Where are you going Santos?"

"I'm going to mind my business Mr. Stone. Around here it's best to move on the need to know basis." He gave Stone a little smile did a complete 180 military style and walked off to his car.

"That's a funny mother fucker," Stone thought to his self. "Fuck it, I came to see Manalo and only him. So, I really don't care who the fuck he is!" Stone jumped in the cherry red 600 Benz with twenty-four-inch rims and took off listening to the voice on the navigation system. "Oh, I'm going to love it down here," He told himself.

The streets were filled with beautiful women walking up and down the strip in catwalk fashion until the moment he got into the expressway. He then started to reflect to how Manalo said he made it to the States a while back. He said, to make it in a small raft the 90-mile distance from Cuba to Miami, he had to throw a close friend of his over board to guarantee his own survival. Shit, it's better that one makes it instead of both dying, don't you think Stone?" Manalo had asked him.

"I never been in such a position Manalo, so I really can't tell you what I would have done. But I most likely would do the same thing if I was in a situation that was life and death." They both shared a small laugh and kept on with the conversation.

For a person to come to this country with nothing and make it the way Manalo did took a lot of work, ruthlessness, focus, ambition, and fearlessness of the repercussions that came with this game. After taking out more than a handful of connected men down in Miami, Manalo is now one of the most powerful connects in south Florida.

Stone then started thinking of New York and his henchmen, Loose, Murder, Pretty boy, B blast, and of course Bump. Their youth, ignorance, and being able to get their hands-on weapons made them the new up and coming in the hood. That's the way it is in all the hoods throughout America. Young guns trying to get a name for themselves, always doing whatever they had to do recklessly. They didn't think about consequences until it was too late for them. That's how it always has been and that's the way it will always be in these streets.

Shit, Stone always kept an extra eye on Bump For the most part. He knew Bump a little over two years when Stone witness Bump fight a man at least 80 pounds more than him. At that it was someone that was not liked at all in the hood. So, it let Bump be a little more embraced by the block. A loudmouth that was always messing with somebody for no apparent reason. The thing about it was that not too many people dare get it popping with this man. But here was Bump, a quiet kid handling his own against this beast it was somewhat a few called a hood David and Goliath story.

Stone seen this kid put combination after combination on this man till the man wanted no more.

Right after the fight Stone approached Bump, "what's good my dude, you did your thing on that bitch nigga Casper."

"Nothing's good. Why what's up?" Bump was very defensive and aggressive at the same time from all the adrenaline he still had flowing through his veins. Stone seen the fire in bumps eyes as if he was ready to get it in again. "Nah it ain't like that my G. Fuck that nigga Casper, he's a piece of shit in my eyes. I don't give two fucks about that fool. The thing is that I always be seeing you on the block and I was just wondering if you live out here, that's all."

Bump stood with his mad dog grill playing his post and said nothing for a few seconds when he saw that Stone wasn't a threat, he let his guards down. "Yeah I live on this sorry ass block."

"It's not that bad, I still can't believe the ass whipping you gave that nigga Primo."

"Believe it because that's what I do", Bump came up boxing in the neighborhood boys club and even attended the golden gloves tournament twice.

Stone reached out his hand to properly introduce his self to Bump, my name is Stone and yours?

Bump ignored Stones hand, "My name is Bump." Bump didn't shake Stones hand to be rude it was just that his hand was broken from all the punching he did on Primo.

"O.K. Bump word of advice out here that fighting shit is done with" Stone went into the small of his back and pulled out a .45 Berretta, Rusty at that. "To many mother fuckers got murdered in these streets because they gave an ass whipping to a person that couldn't handle one. So, if you ask me it's just a waste of time, let's just get it straight to the point, that's the way I feel, you dig?"

Bump didn't like Stones cockiness but still felt this man swagger, "if you say so Stone, I don't doubt it, anyway I want you to meet my team." Blast, Murder, Loose, and Pretty Boy introduced themselves to Stone. "I'm going to be honest I'm a true believer of keeping no more than a hand full on your team but for the new kid on the block I'll make an exception, I mean if you up for it?"

That was two years ago and since then they had come a long way. To the point that Stone is on his way to meet Manalo. He was at the right place at the right time and now he swore he's going to make the best of it. People in the streets just don't get a connect like this on the humble.

Stone reached his destination, as he approached the gate on the estate it opened slowly. Stone couldn't believe his eyes, the size of this house and the land that surrounded it. It was a little over a half of mile to reach Manalo's house once in the estates gate, WOW, it was at least five city blocks to reach the mansion. As he was pulling up, he saw a few Mastiff's and men that was there for one purpose and one purpose only, to protect Manalo. Manalo was waiting patiently for Stone in front of his mansion which resembled the White House a little. He sat comfortably drinking lemonade but who wouldn't when you have so many armed men in your company protecting your investments.

Once out the car Stone walked slowly to Manalo, "Welcome to my home Mr. Stone. I hope that you will enjoy your stay and can get everything you came down to Florida for." Manalo was a tall handsome man with slanted eyes, He is also in very good shape for a man of his age, you can tell that he put hours every week at the gym to maintain his physique.

"I hope so too Manalo; I mean to tell you the truth being around such company I know that I can get what I came down here for."

"You are a smart man and absolutely correct about that Stone. But you need to understand just because I can help you with what you want doesn't mean you will get it. It will all come down to how bad you want it from me and how willing you are to get what you want in life."

"You are 100% correct about that Manalo, He went with the flow because it's true the only shit that matters are that when he leaves, he leaves with what he came down here for."

"O.K then Stone since we are on the same page

how bad you want to get what you came down here for?"

Stone thought for a second because he really was paying attention to Manolo's words. He seen his eyes and they were very intimidating in a sinister way. You could clearly see a person that has no limitations to get what he wants even if it's hurting his own. "I want to get what I came down here for Manolo! I really don't want this trip to be a waste of my time."

They were interrupted by Santos for a second, He walked up to Manolo's side and whispered to his ears so that Stone could not hear the conversation from a couple of feet away. This time Santos had his shirt off and that is when Stone noticed the scar on his neck. "This nigga so lucky to be alive right now with a scar like that", Stone thought. That scars bigger than him, he's only 5'2" a hundred and twelve pounds and that scar is at least a foot long.

"Mr. Stone sorry for the interruption but Santos had some urgent news to tell me that couldn't wait." It was Stones business, but he did not want to tell him yet that there is a crook that is really hurting his business and a lot of other affiliates of his.

"No problem Manalo you have to do what you have to do to keep whatever you have going, going.

I didn't come to be in your way, if anything I think I have something to offer."

"Oh really?" Manalo pushed the chair closer to Stone and gave him his undivided attention with his hands crossed in front of his face as if he was thinking. "Well if it's something I don't do is turn a good opportunity down. Tell me Stone what you have to offer me?"

"I could move anything you put on the table, in the Bronx there's a shortage of coke. So, whoever gets it is going to make a lot of money. I mean to be honest you don't need me I need you! But I tell you one thing for sure there is a lot of money to be made."

"I'm so happy you understand that who needs who. With that I can supply you but there is a little situation that needs handling, I mean if you're up for it Mr. Stone."

"Am I! Just tell me what needs to be done and consider it done. I don't give a fuck what it is as long as it does not degrade my gangster or my manhood." He started to move his legs from side to side from the excitement he was feeling knowing he was so close to get on at the next level.

"I am very glad that you are motivated Stone, but I need to tell you, once you are in this organization with me the only way out is death. I tell you what, you get the job done and I will start you off with twenty kilos."

"So, let's get it done so we can flood my streets Manolo! The quicker it's done the better for me and my team."

Manolo called out Santos name and within seconds you seen Santos rush over to where they were seated.

"Is there a problem Manolo?"

"No there is no problem at all, if anything we have the solution to our little dilemma. But it's only if Stone can get rid of twenty kilos at a time."

Santos looked over at Stone, "So Stone do you think twenty kilos is too much to start off with?"

"Not at all Twenty birds is just right, I think I could get rid of it really quick."

Stone was cut off by Manolo but as he spoke his words were spoken with a tone that made it obvious, he was dead serious. "NO Stone! You cannot believe you can sell twenty kilos you need to know otherwise you are wasting my time and it is not a healthy thing to do. Mr. Stone so can you sell twenty <u>keys</u> without a problem?"

Stone did not even think that one over for a second. "Yes, I can sell anything you bring with the only problems we'll have is counting the cash."

In that case Santos show Stone around town and introduced him to the people he needs to meet. With that there is nothing else to do but see how serious Stone is about getting this money. "Well it was nice talking to you Stone but from here on out we do not speak with words we let our actions do the talking."

"Come on Stone lets go, I will show you where you will be resting your head at during your stay here in Florida."

"Not for nothing Santos I thought you had to take care of some business?"

"I did take care of my business Stone; it was to make sure you traveled alone. But forget about that let me show you how to have a good time down here. What you have coming is a very serious task, so I need to make sure your head is clear." Santos dropped Stone off at the hotel. "Get freshened up Stone I'll be back for you within the hour."

"I'm going to need more than that Santos" Stone said joking. Santos gave the look saying you got to be kidding without words. "It was a joke Santos damn take it easy."

"I don't joke Stone. Life is too serious to play games. So, if you are going to play games you might as well go to the airport and go home right now!"

"Nah I'm good Santos I'll be ready by the end of the hour." Stone grabbed the key and his bags and was on his way to enter the hotel when he was called back by Santos.

"Oh, one more thing, make sure you do not speak to anyone unless I tell you they are o.k. it's very important that you stay under the radar Stone."

"If that is what needs to be done then I won't say a word to anyone." Stone walked off and went directly to his room within the hour Santos was at the front of the hotel waiting. "Come on Stone let's go!" Once in the car Santos had small talk with him about investing properly and learn to move discreet. After about thirty minutes of driving Santos stopped instantly and pointed out the target.

That was when Stone really understood the seriousness of the commitment he just made with Manolo. "Get a real good look at him Stone because this will be the last time, I will be with you until the man is eliminated. Here is a phone number use it only when the pig is gone, and you are already in New York ready to get rich."

Stone got a real good look at him. "I'm good Santos I know how the police officer looks like."

"Good, now let's get you some guns and weed."

Officer Smith was one of the biggest crooks in Miami. He demanded pay from all real money getters and the more Stone trailed him the more Stone saw that he moved like a criminal instead of a person that is supposed to serve and protect under oath.... Smith was a terrorist to those in the life of crime that is why a price tag had been put on him for whoever take his head off. Manolo only jumped on the offer so that his credibility as a drug lord multiplies.

It has been a week and a half and Stone was growing inpatient the way Smith moves made it almost impossible to do it without getting arrested or even killed. The only way that it can get done is if I go and wait for him in his house. Stone told himself.

That is the only time the man put his guards down like nobody has the balls to violate his space. "But what I am going to do with his family Stone", He asked his self. Fuck it because it's not me that put them in harms way by abusing my authority so if anything, it's that pigs' fault.

Smitty got out of work with earning twelve stacks today. Every day he made sure he shook up the willies of the trade but not before picking up dirt on them that could send them to prison for a lifetime. Once you got them by the balls, they will never open their mouths. That's the way he was schooled and that is the way he kept the hustle going.

Officer Smith got to his house the same time as usual ten p.m. but something was not right, all the lights were turned off in his one point two-million-dollar home. Smitty reached for his gun but then changed his mind. She's probably not feeling well he thought out loud. He walked inside his home and locked the door that's when Stone came out of no-where and hit him with a blackjack knocking him out instantly.

Stone was feeling very nervous as he was dragging the officer's body up the stairs. Man, I got to do this shit fast and get up out of here.

His intensions were to make a statement by leaving a message to his fellow officer's but then again, all Manolo wanted was the man dead. Stone then quickly put two slugs into the man head and got the fuck up out of there as fast as a bat does out of hell. It bothered Stone that he just finished eliminating two innocent people. The man wife and son but he knew it was either them or him. He jumped into his car and searched for I-95 north and cruise back to New York.

A day later Stone crossed the George Washington bridge, that's when he started feeling a little relieved. "Wow that was the worst and longest day of my life. I never felt so paranoid in my life", He made that comment to his self. That's when he swore from here on out everything he does is going to be under his terms.

He got home and called Cindy as soon as he got there. "Ma do me a favor come on over and get the car that's in front of my house."

"What do you want me to do with it babes?"

"Just make it disappear without being traced, Thank you so much Sin." That was his nickname for her, "I'll talk to you tomorrow." Stone hung up the phone and went straight to sleep for he'd been up for two days. If anything, Sin was the only person he could trust if there was anybody to truly trust.

Stone was dead asleep but felt Sin inside the crib by her scent alone. That was his road dog, he felt a lot better knowing that the car will never be seen again and knowing her she was going to get a nice amount of change for the Benz. Even though he missed her he stood sleeping cause he was too tired to ask her the hundred.

CHAPTER 4

S tone was reminiscing on how he and the rest of the team have come up, while smoking a blunt of sour diesel. They had nothing but loyalty for one another and with their brave heart mentality they hit the streets hard. They got startup money the American way, by taking it. All it took was a few victims to get them where they wanted to be. Once the goal was reached, they bought nine ounces of coke and got on grind mode. Shit was not all cookies and creams for them in the beginning. There were way too many hustlers out in the streets hustling, fighting, for the money that rotates in the hood. So, the only way to get a better cash flow was to slowly get rid of the competition. It was a long process but in time their executions were all worth it. Stone made sure that they were the only team with product in the entire hood, fuck a corner.

The problem is that having a reliable connect

now and days is very hard to come by. Shit, the main obstacle in the game is to have a consistent supplier that can help you meet your demand to the consumers. So, lots of the time they found themselves with cash but no resources to flip their bread with. That is why Manolo is truly a blessing in disguise for them. Stone finished his blunt and the first thing he did right after that was dial the number Santos gave him to call when he got back to New York.

The phone rang three times when a Spanish man with a heavy accent answered, "Hello who is this"?

The moment Stone heard the person on the other line. He knew it was a voice that didn't sound familiar but at the same time had a similar ascent as Manolo and the others. He was praying that Manolo did not use him to do such a thing and then bail out on his word. Then again if that was the case Stone will have never made it back to New York.

"This is Stone, I'm calling on behalf of Manolo. He told me I can use this number and the receiver of the call will know my purpose for calling".

"Oh, I have been waiting for your call Stone. Give me an address and I'll be there shortly".

Stone gave him the location to his stash house and waited impatiently. No one knew that Stone had this crib apart from Sin and that is the way things are going to stay because now the stakes are too high.

To many people lost their lives for a lot less. After a two hour wait, Eduardo knocked on Stone's door, BOOM, BOOM, BOOM! When Stone opened the door, Eduardo walked in introducing himself, he then told him that the briefcase had twenty kilos of cocaine and three of heroin. Eduardo was a short stocky man with long hair and a full beard.

"The total you owe is six hundred and twenty thousand dollars. The coke is twenty-two and the dope sixty a kilo with that have a nice day and good luck".

The last two words threw Stone off. "Eduardo, can I ask you something, why wish me good luck?"

Eduardo smiled and looked Stone dead in the eyes and told him what it was. "The crown is heavy my boy, real heavy, so once again have a good day". Eduardo walked off and jumped in what looked like a 1988 ford F-150. No one in a right mind frame would even look at Eduardo and think he is holding that much work or involved with that much money.

What the fuck he meant that the crown is heavy? Well whatever it means I bet I will soon find out.

Stone opened the suitcase and that's when he realized the mistake he made. Fuck! He yelled, then he thought what I'm going to do with the dog food! They once told him that good dope sells itself so please let's just hope that's the case here.

Stone got in touch with everyone and told them to meet him in his crib. He grabbed five keys of girl, one of boy and stuffed it in his backpack. That was all his team was going to know they had, for now. Like Biggie said, never let no one know how much dough you hold.

It took everybody about an hour to get there and the ones that got there first wanted to know what the emergency was. The only thing Stone was telling them, was to wait for the rest. Once everybody was in Stone's house he got straight to the point and let them know why it was so important to have them there.

"We got good news and a little bad news but that's only how we look at it. Cause to be honest it can be a real come up. So here it is", Stone dropped the five keys of coke on the table for all to see. All you could hear is the oooohs, and aaaaahss throughout the room. "This is the good news we have a good connect as of today".

"But the bad news is this", that's when he dropped the key of dope. "He expects us to also get rid of this", pointing at the kilo of heroin.

"What the fuck is this"? Murder cut in grabbing the kilo of heroin confused.

"What the fuck you think it is?! This shit is that boy. We going to step our game up and get some of that Dope money from here on out. What I'm going to do is put Blast and Bump responsible for the distribution of the dog food. While the rest take care of the easy work and get rid of the coke".

"I need for ya to understand, we are in a lot of debt but once paid the rewards are going to be off the hook. There is not going to be a nigga out here that is going to fuck with our paper. But we have to be really careful with all the haters out here counting other people's money, ya dig? All kind of people are going to be on to us. Especially the ones that are going to be affected by our clientele".

Bump was not comfortable with the way Stone always said what was going to happen like he was Fidel Castro or something.

"Why do I have to be responsible for getting rid of the dope when I don't know shit about it"?

"We talk about that later Bump in private, just see how the game is before you protest. Right now, let me cook some of this shit up so we can save the streets from this drought". Out of everybody in the team it was always Bump that had to play the devil's advocate. To the others that was just Bump, but to Stone, Bump was becoming independent and badly wanted to grow on his own.

Stone went into the kitchen with a key of cocaine to do what he does best. (Wake up in the morning with my wrist doing circles!) He got a Pyrex pot, a cereal box size baking soda, ice on standby and a fork so he can whip the shit out of it. While he chef the coke up, the crew smoked weed and popped shit on how they were going to do this and that with all the money they about to make. Loose already had a house and the man had not even sold a gram of coke yet.

Stone bust open the key right after he did his best breaking it up. He sat the pot on the stove on low flames, threw in two hundred and fifty grams of coke and another ninety of baking soda. He then added a little water and whipped the fork in circular motions as the contents melted into one. With the heat and the water, the coke got into a paste form he then added more baking soda and whipped for about another three minutes nonstop like a baker would whip eggs and milk into a cake batter. Then he put some cold water and ice to harden it.

After it was ready Stone weighed it to know for sure what came back from it all. Three hundred and forty grams, "oh we in there" he told himself. When everything was all said and done Stone had pulled thirteen hundred and sixty grams out of one key. Even with extras the crack was hard and difficult to break. He walked into the living room and dropped everything into Loose hands.

"Yo Loose give me back thirty-four stacks for

this". "There's nothing out there right now so charge thirty a gram". "At the end of the day you'll get damn near seven G's for you and believe me there is a lot more where that came from".

He then turned to Murder and gave him a key of coke. "You sell the raw to the masses while Loose sells the cook up". "But do me a favor don't waste your time with dudes spending a few hundred, sell weight!"

"I got no problem with that my G believe me I know what to do". Loose and Murder always took orders well, for all they knew they were the youngest out the team. So, they got up out of there to do what they had to do without questions. To them it really didn't matter for they are making money that they never had. So, whatever had to be done they did it only because they are thankful to be in this opportunity.

Bump was not cool with the fact that it was not him to oversee the white girl. "If anything, Stone should have let me take care of business", he told his inner self. I swear I'm really getting tired of this nigga Stone, Bump thought. He wanted to go on his own, but he knew the time was not right, he had no connect and his money was not up yet to reach the point of independence.

Once Loose, Pretty boy, and Murder left Stone turned his attention to Bump and Blast. "I was gonna let ya take care of the coke, but I never expected to get dog food from my connect". "This dope shit takes a lot of responsibility to maintain, it's a delicate drug but in return it would make us rich overnight if we do the right thing with it". "I'm counting on you two only because I feel ya are the more responsible ones and the more mature out the team". "Anybody could sell coke and crack, but it takes a hustler to sell this shit right here", Stone said while lifting the brick for the two to see.

"I don't know nothing about this dope shit Stone"! Bump said with an attitude like if it was a curse to have this much dope.

"Me either Bump but what the fuck you wanted me to do turn down the coke cause I don't have the customers at the moment". "Trust me this is some grade A shit that's gonna get us a lot of money".

"So, what you want us to do Stone", Blast cut in.

"Flood the streets with that poison, believe me it's going to sell itself. Just have someone cut the shit up and whoever wants to get money let them as long as you know the persons background and what they about. If the moment comes that somebody plays with our bread, I'll take care of it myself and you know how I do".

"Say no more", Blast took the key of dope cause he knew where to take it. "Come on Bump let's get the fuck up out of here and start getting this bread". "China I'm gonna need you to come with me so we don't look so suspicious coming out of the building".

"Nigga please just let me know your sorry ass is scared and you need a real bitch to do your work you punk mother fucker".

"Man shut the fuck up and take this shit, what the fuck you think you around us for, to just look pretty and be spoiled rotten".

"You didn't say please that is why I have not moved a finger yet and if I tell you why I'm around your sorry ass might get pissed off".

"Come on China stop playing so much and let's get the fuck up out of here". They always went at it, but they had nothing but love for one another.

Cindy finally got some alone time with Stone which made her happy. These are rare times, so she always makes the best of it. As he sat quietly, watching T.V., thinking about how he was going to strategies everything. She went into the bathroom and took off her clothes. She bought herself very sexy lingerie in hope that they would of have some alone time. She sprayed herself with her trademark perfume, Chanel no.5. She walked out the bathroom and walked towards Stone giving him a seductive look. Shaking her hips side to side as if she was on the catwalk modeling for Victoria's secret.

Stone knew what Cindy wanted but right now his mind was on paper. "Not now babes, please my mind is on other things and that will distract me. At this moment the only thing I want to do is get the money I owe. I am the one responsible to pay what is owed for this work. It's a lot of money involved to pay them off sweetheart. People like them are vicious and will not hesitate to do anything to us."

"I'm not trying to hear that bull shit pappi! My ass has been waiting for you to get back from wherever the fuck you were at and now you talking this money shit. You better take your fucking clothes off before I tear them off Pappi, I'm not playing". She grabbed him and forcefully started to take his clothes off.

Stone loves that about Cindy, she never takes no for an answer. Whatever it is she won't stop till she gets it. Most woman are relentless like that with the man they want to get, but Sin was like that with everything now.

"You not going to stop harassing, are you babes"?

Cindy gave Stone a Kool-Aid smile showing off her perfect teeth. "You know I'm not daddy", that moment Cindy reached for Stones belt without him protesting one bit.

Stone loves Cindy to death but for some reason

he always held his emotions back. Like loving is a sign of weakness, well at least in his world, Sin knew the time though. There's no way in the world she would love a person that does not love her back, especially after she been through in life. She took her time with him working up an erection in seconds. "Since you are not in a mood just sit there and do nothing". That was a lie, she knew his horny ass couldn't resist her. "My smell alone gets this nigga hard" she thought to herself.

Stone first caressed her bubble butt and spanked her making one of her cheeks sting. He then kissed her ass he caressed the small of her back. He worked her clothes as she rushed on taking his clothes off. They undressed and Sin jumped on him cowgirl style grinding her pussy to his hard on. He then slid her G-string to the side and guided his head into her opening. It didn't matter how many times they had sex she was always tight even when wet. She first rode him slowly until she was able to take the pain. After a minute or so the pain turned into pleasure and she rode him wildly. Within minutes Stone flipped her over and took charge of the whole situation.

They had an hour-long session of passionate sex which left Stone forgetting about everything but worrying about catching his breath. Stone looked into her eyes, kissed her lightly, then told her what every female wants to hear the man they love tell them, "I love you baby".

Blast, China, and Bump got to his apartment the only thing on his mind at that moment is to see his father. Blast's pops was an all-out dope fiend but back in the days he did his numbers in the streets. He ran strong with a lot of street legends and was practically hood rich. Everywhere he went people knew him and gave him the respect he deserved. That was before, now that he fell to the God that kept him rich for so long, no one even knows he exist.

"Yo Bump do me a favor, I need you to go with China and buy a few things that we need to get the ball rolling while I get my pops, so that I can talk to him".

"What do you want me to go out there and get Blast"?

"Hold on let me get a piece of paper and a pen so that I can write it up for you". Blast made a list of what he needed:

- A large coffee grinder machine
- A case of wax bags
- A case of manita bars
- Masks
- An adjustable stamper with ink
- A few metro cards

- Measuring spoons
- Scotch tape
- Strainers
- A large mirror, so they can do all the cutting on it
- A box of swishers and a few twenties of Cush.

"Why we got to go through all this bullshit to get money? This dope shit is crazy man, I don't like dealing with so much shit. I tell you, Stone should have let me just deal with the Coke instead of having me experimenting with this heroin".

Bump always had a thing or two to say about everything. It was as if all the labor had to be beneficial for him or he did not want a part of it. To Blast, Bump was not a team player and people like that always waited for the opportunity so that they can capitalize for themselves. In his mind, Bump already crossed them all, he was waiting for was Stone's order and Blast swore he would take him out instantly.

Two hours later they got the news from Blast's pops that this was the best shit he had in years. "You going to kill the competition out there with this", as pops spoke Bump laughed cause he was in cloud nine leaning like one of those V-8 commercials.

"Just be really careful with this hustle, it attracts

the worst of everything. Just make sure none of ya let the money get into your thick-headed skulls". As he spoke, he scratched his arm leaving red spots on his ashy skin.

"Why you always got to say something out the ordinary pops"?

Pops looked his son dead in the eyes with a grave stare. "It's a magnet for feds, stick up kids, and most of all betrayal my son. There's a lot of money in this, money that at times, a mother fucker never seen and with that people do crazy shit. It's one's inner demons that fucks shit up when shit is going good for them. If together is the way you got here make sure it's together that you rise and when you on top, together is how you stick. Otherwise everything that you work for will go in vain, it's crazy while you on the top at times it gets lonely because when you get there you find out you can't trust no one".

"I wish a nigga would try some shit with us". Blast got up from where he was sitting and went to his room for a second coming back with a duffel bag. Blast showed his pops the bag of arms he had in the closet filled with Macs 11's, .45's, 9mm's, even two grenades but pops was not impressed with that.

"What good is all these guns when this game is built out of back stabbers". "You'll never see it coming from the back no matter how many guns you got because it usually comes from someone that is close to you. The only thing I could tell you son is to never trust anyone if you feel a guy is cool watch him more cause most agendas are hidden".

Blast knew that pops knows what he's talking about, so he won't put it past him. His life turned inside out when his best friend left him for dead over ten lousy stacks. The foul shit regarding the entire situation was Momma Love was in on it. They tried to get him for all, but he was smart enough to not even trust his baby mommas.

Just thinking of the past breaks Blast heart to know it was his own mom that tried to make him a bastard. "Enough of this pops, make this shit happen, cut it up so we can bag it, stamp it up, and get this money".

"Got it, I also want to tell you that I got a hell of a clientele my damn self. Make sure I get my share of the pie son. Dope fiend and all, I'm going to get me some paper".

"O.K. pops but please one thing at a time you make me nervous. Take care of this first then we talk about hustling a little later. You know I don't like that shit when you start talking all fast. You know I know you real well pops, I seen you talk people out of their socks out here so I ain't gonna let you do it to me".

"You got it mother fucker!", just that fast daddy cool got all angry and felt a bit violated by what his son told him. "You also know that I don't like no sperm of mine disrespecting me". He looked at his son like he wanted to whip his ass. But pops know it has been a long time ago since he even tried to discipline him and right now it was too late in the relationship to even try.

Blast had no choice but to laugh at those words that came out of his dad mouth. When pops saw that his son found that humorous, he couldn't hold it in either, he broke down laughing. "I love you so much son you never treated me like a dope fiend. No matter how much that monkey had a grip on me".

"How can a man treat all he has in this world like a dope fiend? It would make me worst of a person, what kind of a man would I be, if I can't respect who gave me life".

Pops cried from those words, but he held his tears inside. "I would do anything for you son the time will come where I won't fail you. I know I have been failing you all my life cause of my addiction, but you will see. When you least expect it, I will be there my son".

"Come on pops please let's not get all sensitive and get this shit done there is money to be made". With that pops left it at that, but he made an oath with his self that he was going to step his game up.

CHAPTER 5

The next day Blast went to Stone's house first thing in the morning. All excited ready to tell him the good news his pops have gave him concerning the dog food. He also had an ounce of that sour so they can smoke. It is like a tradition when they politic on what goes on in the streets and contemplate the next move. Smoke weed, play chess and build on how they can get more paper out the hood with minimizing the obstacles.

"Yo Stone that work is fire I'm telling you, everybody is loving it". "My pops did his thing with it and got me a few spenders that promise to spend a lot more cash once they get more feedback from other customers. I'm telling you; I got a real good feeling on this dope shit bro. I think this what's going to take us to the next level".

"I told you Blast all we got to do is be patient and watch who we deal with and the sky is the limit from here on out".

"You not lying bro, what my pops did was bag up some fire and put different stamps so that nobody would know it's coming from the same source. He then cut some and recompressed it to sell it as weight to those that refuse to take percentage. So, if you want the fire, get them bundled up already. Shit we got it heavy so it's nothing to give mother fuckers fifty percent for the bundles".

"You sure it will work like that Blast; I mean it's a lot of work for us. I don't know if you are willing to be bagging up all day".

"Truthfully speaking I got faith in my pops, that he is going to get the stamps known out there. The nigga is not a slouch, yeah, he gets high and all, but still he's always taking care of his business. Besides that, old man is a veteran in this dope shit. Now as far as stamping and bagging all day I won't mind as long as the money is coming in".

"How the fuck you know Blast that your dad is good? Your ass never conducted any type of business with him".

"You know why Stone because I never needed for shit, that's why I say that. He also made like twelve stacks last night and promise to make more than that today".

"Get the fuck out of here", Stone was impressed by the quick results Blast showed in distributing the drug, especially on short notice. "If it's like that we going to be rich in no time". Stone smiled and showed his perfect teeth, to someone else that would be a first-time thing but not to Blast he knew Stone was a good man at heart. It's just that you must bring out the animal in these streets.

"Word up Stone, pop Dukes also said that's chump change to what he is capable of doing. He let me know dope fiend or not the streets are going to want to do business with him cause of the potency of the material".

"Shit if it's like that let him rock with you. Let your old man get that guap with us. God knows he is in real need of making his own instead of you supporting his habit".

"That is not going to happen Stone, I'm just going to deal with my pops accordingly. We need to remember that my dad like to get high of that poison.

I don't know if I can deal with me being the downfall of my own flesh and blood. Come one day I might find him overdosed slumped somewhere with all the money he will be making with us".

"You know him a lot more than I do Blast. Now pass that blunt I want to get high too". Stone reach for the blunt took a few pulls then changed the subject after he coughed up a storm from the weed.

"Oh shit" Stone yelled excited; you don't see what just happened pointing at the chess board.

"Nah what"?

"Check mate nigga that's what! Now pay me my hundred dollars Blast".

Blast paid Stone the buck highly upset, "Here take your hundred punk ass dollars! I can't believe your bum ass beat me again".

"Fuck you talking about Blast I have been beating you since I first taught you this game". Looking at Blast get upset once again from losing all the time had Stone in tears. For some reason every time Blast got upset Stone could not prevent from laughing. "You my fucking dog Blast, I love you to death, From the cradle to the grave my brother".

Even though Blast loved Stone the same, that split second all Blast can think about was what his father was talking to him last night about. "Don't trust no one in this game my son you will never see a back stabber coming, never forget son all agendas are hidden." He quickly erased the idea out of his head, Nah, not my nigga Stone he told himself.

A few weeks have passed, and Bump was on the grind hard today. But one of the people he spoke to and conducted business with was X. X got in touch with him the second he found out that Bump was dealing a nine and a half in the hood. Even though

Bump knew how Stone felt about X, he went against the grain and dealt business with him. This time being more comfortable with him he met up in X crib to discuss numbers. They just started dealing with one another but believe it or not they shared the same feelings about Stone. It's ironic how they can have more in common with one another then Bump did with Stone. Besides he did not see in X what Stone saw in him. Giving him the reason to dislike him so much more.

"So, Bump how much work you can get me in one shot. I mean you already know my flow is ridiculous and my paper is right. Let's get this money and cut the games out, come on Bump let's get it"!

"I know you got a pretty good flow and your paper right but that's not the problem".

"So, what is the problem Bump that we are having right now," X asked. "You in the game to get rid of shit not hold on to it till it goes bad. What are you hustling backwards", X shot at Bump.

"Come on X who the fuck you think you talking too", Bump quickly got upset. "The only dilemma we have right now is that you and Stone do not get along". "If ya two were on good terms the amount of work your hands would be touching right now would be unlimited. But since you two do have a problem in which I have no clue why. Then the supply in which you get from me will be limited cause I can't go over Stone head".

"Man, I don't want to hear all that", X said getting tired of the bullshit. "All I want to know is how to get my hands on enough of that shit to meet the demand that I have right now in the hood".

"The only way I see you getting some of this is if you put your money up and straight up buy". He did not want to lose X as a customer so what he will do is get him what they cut and compressed. "Other than that, I can't help you no more then I already am. You need to understand that man is not a game, if he ever finds out about our dealings were both as good as dead".

"I'm not trying to hear that shit; you talk as if that bitch ass nigga don't bleed."

"Oh, he bleeds but you got to outsmart him, X. Is no way in the world you will be able to run up on him and kill the bastard. Especially now, that man is very hard to be spotted and if you see him, he is never alone or unarmed".

"How the fuck your ass talkin' about that nigga like that, it's as if you are scared of the man." "Are you scared of him?" X spoke to Bump highly upset.

"Don't be a fool X, I'm not scared of him! But I also didn't come here to premeditate his death, we met up so we can discuss business. So, if you want to do business call me, you know how to get it, get your money up and buy once a week. Other than that our dealings should not be obvious to anyone other than ourselves".

X felt a little disrespected by the way Bump spoke to him in his own house. But at this moment he needs Bump to get him what he wants. "That's fine Bump I'll call you when I put my money together".

"Do that!" Bump left the crib to go see Stone and for a second, the thought of what Stone would do with him if he ever found out his dealings with X got him a bit nervous. The funny shit was that even though he knew the outcome he still wanted to be his own man doing his own thing.

It took a little over three weeks to get Manolo's money together. They had made arrangements that Santos would come to New York and pick up Manolo's money only if Stone would pay for all expenses, which he was more than happy to do for Stone. Shit after what happened in Miami it would take a lot for Stone to ever set foot there again. Stone waited for Santos and showed him the same hospitality that Santos showed him when the foot was on the other shoe. Stone was glad that all went well but did not know what amount to expect from them this time around. As far as the amount of kilo's in which he will get now goes.

Arriving at Kennedy Airport Stone waited patiently for Santos happy that he did not have to leave New York. He told him exactly where he was going to be, so it was not hard to find Stone. "Hey Santos, how you doing"?

"I'm doing great! You need to know I love this city. I have been to New York many times but never to deal business of this kind".

"A lot of people love New York but being from here, your feeling towards the Big Apple changes over the years. It amazes how this city is so rich but so many people suffer from poverty. It lets you know that the government doesn't give a fuck about the poor. It's on you to do whatever you can to break the chains of financial enslavement".

"Look with all due respect Stone I did not fly all the way to New York to discuss our political differences. I came to have a good time and take back what belongs to Manolo. Right now, I can eat like a champ why don't we just get some food and get better acquainted".

"That sounds like a plan, is there any place in particular that you want to eat at"?

"Not really Stone let's just go to a place that is quiet and the food is great".

"We can go to City Island then, this time of the year there aren't too many people there". They went to one of the more upscale restaurants there and took their time ordering.

They ordered their food and Stone could not believe how this small man ate so big. Santos saw how Stone looked at him, for some reason every time he dined with a person for the first time they'll be in shock at how he can eat so much.

"They say the size of a man is determined by how his appetite is", Santos told Stone with a mouth full of food.

"In that case you must be a giant Santos because you eat like a N.F.L lineman I swear to you". Santos could not hold his food in from Stones sarcasm in which it made Santos laugh. He spat food all over the table they were eating only missing Stone by inches.

"Oh, you a comedian for real aren't you Stone, I haven't laughed that hard in God knows how long Stone. Now truthfully speaking Stone I want you to know that as long as you are a good business associate with Manolo I am here for you. I say that to all our associates but you, there is something different about you. For some reason I see loyalty in you and that makes me want to be there for you even more. Besides I already know that you are willing to sacrifice everything for your cause".

"Thank you, Santos it's appreciated and makes me happy to know I have your support. I think everything is good right now so as long as you just keep bringing in that work you gave me; you will be doing enough".

"Yeah but that does not mean that it will stay like that in the long run. For some reason life is never trouble free when you make a lot money. Truthfully speaking how you think Manolo was able to stay on top of the game? Problems are always around the corner when you about your business".

"I don't know how Manolo stayed on top Santos, to be honest I never gave it much thought. But now that we talking about it tell me how he did he stay on top"?

"He had me on his team Stone, the good thing about it is so can you. What I'm trying to tell you is that for the right price I can get anything done and believe me I mean anything. There is not a person out in these streets that could stand up against a man like me. What I do I do well, and you have the privilege of having me at your service whenever it's needed".

"So curiously speaking what would it cost me to have you at my service? I learn that everything has its price and that is a lesson that was learned a long time ago".

"That my friend would determine on how much money you have already made and how bad you want it done. But enough of this chit chat, Stone I'm going to enjoy myself for the next two days. I'll see you on my next trip to New York Stone if all goes well".

Santos picked up the suitcase that had the money then tucked the envelope that was his personal earnings for the trip in his jacket. He looked around before putting it in his inside pocket making sure no one was observing.

"Once again have a nice day and I am looking forward to seeing you real soon".

Stone had called a cab that was waiting outside the restaurant for the past ten minutes. Santos got up from his chair picked up the briefcase. Nodded his head to Stone and left the place without ever looking back or saying anything to Blast, who he was sitting with them the entire time.

CHAPTER 6

For the next couple of months things could have not gone any better. They all made more money than they believed they would ever see in a lifetime out of these streets. Shit even X was happy with the share of the pie that he was getting. The only thing that bothered him was that his dealings with Bump still had to be discreet so that Stone would not find out he was eating with them. He made it clear numerous times that dealing with X is prohibited no matter how much money he is willing to spend or brings to the table. So, Bump knew to not let X get to big but still feed him more then what he usually was accustomed too.

Stone made it a primary rule to keep the flossing to a minimum only cause they were making way too much money. That should be a rule for longevity to all hustler in the hood. So, anything that would bring prosperity to his team would be a rule for them that they would have to live by. It has happened way too many times in the past to other people for them to make the same mistakes. Why floss your money while you still trapping when the only vibes you will get from others would be negative? There is way too many haters and snitches out there to brand yourself as a boss hog.

Stone never forgot when he was told by Eduardo that the crown is heavy. He learned in time to isolate his self from the rest but more importantly from outsiders. That would be the only way that he can conduct proper business with his friends and keep everything in order. If not, the game would be all over him instead of him being on top of his game. It's a jungle that can consume you if you are not careful. So even though he wanted to do things that he always wanted to do when he didn't have money. He had to play it safe for now and get low for the mean time. What good is to make that much money too then spend it on legal fees cause you are out there and get caught up.

He was in the crib enjoying a ménages with Cindy and China when he received a call from Pretty boy. When he picked up the phone all he can hear was someone crying hysterically on the other side of the line. He knew something was not right and always tried to prepare himself for one of these calls. The streets are a battlefield that you will have to fight for your survival from the moment you get in it. That battle does not stop until you are dead, in jail, or just smart enough to walk away. But then again in jail or prison a different more intense battle begins.

"Yo Pretty what the fuck is happening!" Cindy saw Stones face expression and knew something was wrong.

Pretty had to catch his breath first before giving Stone the news. "They killed him man, they killed Loose, Stone our boy Loose is not with us no more". He cried out loud hurt from the loss of his best friend. The two did everything together, shopping, fucking bitches, getting money, they even live together.

Stone couldn't believe his ears; he was just hoping that he heard wrong, so he asked Pretty again to confirm what he thought he just heard him say.

"What did you say to me Pretty", Stone asked numb from the news. "Tell me you just didn't say what I thought you just did man". Stone asked even though he knew what Pretty was saying.

"You didn't hear me the first time, Loose is dead Stone". Pretty yelled into the phone tired of repeating the bad news.

"Don't say nothing else over the phone bro just come to the house and give me more details of what happened face to face". It was as if a piece of Stone was just ripped out of his chest. To lose a love one by violence, death never affected Stone personally. He was always around murder, but he was a giver of it not a receiver of the pain it brings.

When Stone hung up the phone Cindy was all on top of him trying to find out what was the reason that Pretty called. She knew something was wrong by the face that he made while he was on the phone, for she knew Stone better then Stone knew his self.

"Baby what's wrong, I know shits not right. Who got hurt?" Cindy asked worried as the tears rolled down her face.

"Nobody's got hurt Sin, they killed Loose", she did a double take not believing what he just said.

The words that Stone told her got her and China all hysterical. In a way it upset Stone only because this is part of the game and they acted as if everything is going to be peaches and cream all the time. He knows the game and seen death all his life to know it could happen to any of them at any time. That was his reason for always being on top of his team, so that they could take the game serious and don't get caught slipping.

"Calm the fuck down girls please I got to think. Ya know the game we in, every day will not be a good one for us, so we need to take in the good with the bad. That is why I tell everybody to move a certain way, so that shit like this can be prevented.

Damn Loose", His boy had come up a long way to end so soon for him. To be honest he was the only one that was showing off his money, with the jewelry, cars, women, and always buying out bars in clubs. He had told him to tone it down but Loose didn't listen to what Stone had to say. Now look how it ended, some jealous mother fucker took his life, a dead jealous mother fucker at that! Cause whoever did this will have to pay in full.

Pretty came over and told him what had happened with Loose. He told him about his dealings with some Brooklyn cats and that was who he went to see. They didn't know too many people out in Brooklyn so the only reason Loose would go there would be to see him.

"Do you know who they are Pretty and where they from", Stone asked. "Tell me anything that could help me get them bitch mother fuckers", Stone asked punching his palm and curling his lip.

"I know what they look like and where they from, but I don't know them as good as Murder do".

"Say no more my G, go and tell the news to the rest of the team Cindy, China go with them also I need time for myself".

"Are you sure babes I can stay with you if you want me too", Cindy protested.

"What did I just say to you Cindy", Stone

remarked, agitated just cause he hold her a second ago to go with Pretty. Stone waited for them to leave so that he can do what he wanted to do the moment he heard the news. Even though death is part of the game losing a love one is always hard, he suppressed his emotions till there was no one around him then vented. That's some shit he never did in front of anyone. In his mind crying was a sign of weakness at least that is how others will look at it as, he thought. But the truth of the matter is that men cry as well.

Stone felt guilty regarding Looses death, to him he had some of the blame only because he introduced him to the lifestyle that they chose to live and die by. "I promise you my brother they will pay in full for what they did."

The very next day they met up in Pretty's house to mourn, smoke, drink, and reflect on all the good times they shared with Loose. After about an hour or so Stone asked Murder to give him a second in privacy to discuss a few matters. They went into a bedroom to speak on what had happened to their friend.

"Let's get straight to the point Murder, what happened to Loose? I mean more then what is obvious to us already concerning his death".

"Stone, he met some niggas from Brooklyn at a club a couple of weeks ago. I guess it was evident to them that Loose was getting heavy paper in the game. Stone you know how Loose like to shine all the time doing it like he was getting rapper money or something".

"Yes, I know Murder, but I don't want to hear what I already know. Who are they, where are they from, and how could I get my hands on them fools"? It was Murder's job to be the shadow and keep an eye on everything that does not look right.

"All I know is that they some dudes that be Cripping somewhere in Flatbush Avenue. I personally only know one of them that goes by the name of Classic. The others I don't know cause we never got to get a good look at them or even get to meet".

"That was all I wanted to know, there is nothing else that has to be said. As long as when the time comes you can point them out. Now make sure that Loose has an appropriate burial and his moms can get all the help she needs with it. Other than that we all know pay back is a bitch and we are going to make sure we get it for Loose".

"Got you my brother, I am going to take care of it for you". Those words made Murder feel secured knowing Stone will do the same for him. God forbid death ever meets him in the streets. That is a rare quality in the streets today where you have comrades that hold you down when you are down and out.

Stone called Santos that instant to let him know that he will take him on the offer he had proposed to him months ago. As far as ever needing his services to clean problems up.

"Just give me the call Stone and I'll be there A.S.A.P. He did not like to talk over the phone so that was all he was going to say". It's about time that Stone got into some shit, now I can make cash the best way I know how, he thought to himself.

"Let me gather up the accurate information that is needed then I'll get back at you". Stone did not want to sound too desperate; he remember what Santos told him relating to the price he charges to get the job done. It all depends on how bad you really want it done. Those were the exact words Santos told Stone when he asked him how much he will be charged.

"Just do that Stone and I will be on standby ready to go to New York, whenever you need me to".

"Do that because it will be real soon that I will be needing your services".

Classic robbed five keys from Loose and for that much he knew that the only way to pull it off was by taking Loose's life. How the fuck a man could be so laid back when there was so much at stake. Classic could not understand it, that's why getting him crossed his mind so quickly. The man for the most part came alone without a strap for worse case scenarios. So Loose recklessness change Classics financial status in one second. All it took was the pull of the trigger and a snatch of a bag. But he gave the man credit he did not budge when he told Classic to do what he got to do. He looked him straight in his eyes and did not plead one bit as his goon had Loose under the barrel. He kept eye contact with him until his life left his body and still in a creepy way Loose kept staring at him.

Classic was popping bottle after bottle waving cash around like he was a ball player that just finish signing a fresh contract. Every member of his team was under the influence of alcohol, popping molly, weed, or something. All the females from the hood were around so you know the dudes is going to follow. To be honest everyone was around them for the simple fact that Classic bought the bar out. Especially when many did not have it to drink the way they were that day. It was a happy get together for everybody from their block. It's been a long time since someone has balled this hard in the hood for the hood.

Murder and Stone waited patiently on his block determined to see Classic. Murder took Stone to Flatbush and seen a familiar face that was with Classic the one time Murder came with Loose.

"I saw that nigga before with Classic, but I don't

see Classic out here Stone. He is definitely one of the guys that was with classic. I'll put my life on that", Murder said pointing at some dude dressed in a Pittsburg Steelers jersey and some all black Chuck Taylors.

That was all that Murder had to say to Stone to get him amped up. Stone got out the car and walked towards Joker getting straight to business. "Excuse me young gun you know where I can get some bud", Stone asked him like all was good and well.

"Yeah, I got some bud right here for you cuz", going into his pocket. Joker never seen Stone pull out the forty calibers on him until it was too late, Stone got the drop on Joker aiming his gun directly between his eyes.

"Get the fuck in the car or I'll blow your fucking head off". Stone strong armed him grabbing Joker by the back of his neck, pressing the barrel to his temple as he threw him into the car.

"Chill the fuck out man I did nothing to you", Joker yelled not knowing where this was coming from. "Who the fuck you think you are coming to my hood doing what you are doing! Like there is not going to be no repercussions for your actions". Stone wasted no time to let this fool know he meant business. Stone damn near broke the pistol with the force he used to hit him in the back of the head. Blood gushed out viciously out of Joker's head. To Stone surprise the bastard was still awake, this hardheaded mother fucker Stone thought.

"Young gun if you don't want to die right now, tell me where the fuck Classic is". I lie to you not if you think you are not going to say a word think again cause I swear on my mother's eyes I'll torture it out of you."

That instant Joker knew what this was all about, "please don't kill me", Joker pleaded looking into this man eyes. Crack! Stone hit Joker again but this time it was over his mouth knocking his front teeth out.

"AAHHH…." Joker moaned in pain while the blood gushed out of his mouth rapidly ruining the interior of the car.

"I'm going to be honest with you kid, the only way you are not dying tonight is if Classic dies for you, So don't be a dead hero and worship your life. Now tell me where that piece of shit is at right now. Otherwise your momma is going to bury you by the end of the week in a closed casket".

Joker knew the man in front of him meant business, so he had no choice but to tell him. It's either talk or hold your peace forever. He knew it would be today that he will meet his maker.

"He's a couple of blocks down Flatbush in a sports bar partying up a storm. You can't miss him he's the one making the place shine".

"Are you sure? I don't want to have to come back here and skin you alive boy". Stone looked in the man eyes and knew he would not lie to him and chance his life. He was too scared to even think of giving him a lie.

"I'm not lying he's in there, I swear to God, please don't kill me" he pleaded. Joker knew the amount of people that were in there partying and the chances of this man getting Classic would be one to a hundred.

"Good looking young gun now get the fuck up out of here, before I change my mind". Stone opened the door and kicked Joker out of the car. Joker thought he was safe and out of harm's way as he was getting up from the concrete floor. The problem was he never paid any attention to Blast and Bump chilling on the front of the building waiting for him.

"Thank you, man, thank you for not killing me". Even though Stone was already gone he thanked him for giving him another shot at life. He ran off towards the building with a bloody face but still loving life. Joker was relieved that tonight he was not meeting his maker and live to see another day. If them dudes knew better, they would have killed him cause it was him that shot Loose the day he got murdered. As Stone drove off Joker just knew he was good and out of harm's way.

"I can't believe these stupid mother fuckers let me

live" he thought to himself. Joker ran to his building in hope that he can have enough time to get his burner and get to the lounge in time. No one was out here on the block. So, he ran to get his burner to make it appear like he is the one to save the day. Instead of directing the wolves to Classic. As Joker ran into his building lobby, Bump dead armed him almost putting him to sleep. Not again, that is what he was thinking as he was falling to the ground.

"Now get the fuck up and don't say a word", Bump lift him by his braids. "Take me to the trap house, I swear to everything you make a funny move I'm putting this clip in you. As Bump displayed his gun to Joker. "You faggot mother fuckers think you could do my man dirty and get away with it. Not in this lifetime especially to niggas like us". He laughed lightly savoring this very moment of revenge.

That instant Joker knew Classic done fucked up on the wrong people. He seen these men eyes and it was only one thing that you can see, DEATH! "Look man I didn't do anything", Joker was doing his best to plead for his life. So, to show him that they didn't give two fucks! Bump pistol whipped him three times Breaking the left side of his jaw splitting his face. The blow made a three-inch gash across his cheek bone. At this point there was blood everywhere. Joker was drenched in his own blood from head to toe. They were trying to get him to the crib. but the bitch came out of him. He yelled bloody murder for all tenants to hear his pleads. As if that was going to save him from Bump and Blast playing their part for the night.

"Please... somebody help me they going to kill me", Joker yelled from the top of his lungs out of fear.

Bump could not take it no more. he knew that somebody heard him. So, he had to finished him off then and there. He put the entire clip in the dude face like he promised. It's always good to keep a round or two when riding out just in case a person ever wants to be a hero. You need to fire a warning shot to give you a better chance at getting away.

"Why the fuck you killed him, Bump?". Blast asked only because he wanted to get some money back from the loss, they took. "What good is it to war so much without getting a profit".

"Fuck that nigga", Bump wanted to get shit done and get the fuck out of Brooklyn. He ignored whatever Blast had to say now. All he did was run out the building, get in the car, turn the ignition on, and waited for Blast to get in the car. It pissed Blast off, but this was not the time to discuss feelings. Believe me though we'll have time for that. Blast got in the car and Bump stepped on it taking them back to the Boogie Down in silence. As of late the two have been having little fall outs over the dumbest shit. To the point where both are getting tired of the nonsense. It will be a matter of time in which this relationship will turn sour. They are both men with strong personalities sharing different views.

Stone wanted to kill Classic the moment he spotted him in the sports bar. To be looking at the man that killed Loose, his comrade, was killing him. However, he knew he did not have the fire power to pull it off at this moment. The place was jammed pack, it must have been at least a hundred nigga's with blue flags, Cripping. At that moment Stone wish he had a pair of grenades.

So that Classic's actions will affect all his peoples by receiving fragments of metal from the miniature pineapples. The real shit is that wishing wasn't going to get any one of these busters killed. Seeing these bitches party at the expense of Loose made Stone hate Crips so much more. Into the point where he would like to see all that bang this structure, die slow.

"Yo Murder we got to get this mark another time. It's no way in the world that we can get out of here alive if we start firing. We did not get searched coming in and we strangers to this place. God knows who else is holding burners up in here that are locals."

They had no choice but to get up out of there for the mean time. It killed him to see him there and not be able to do anything now. His rage got the best of him as his face curled up not being able to control his emotions. As he was leaving out the lounge towards his car his mind changed. He couldn't leave without doing anything to them in retaliation to Loose.

"I can't leave without doing something to these people up in here". "If you want to leave, I understand Murder. But I just am not going to get up out of here without doing something".

Murder could not believe he told him that bullshit, "Say that to one of your bitches my brother". "I'm not hearing it, you my dude Stone, I came with you and the only way that I will go home is if you come back with me". "Otherwise we are here together from the cradle to the grave", as he said that he beat on his chest mimicking a Gorilla.

Stone knew he was safe with Murder and if not safe then still he will have someone riding with him till the end. Murder is known to say what he means and means what he says. They sat patiently, waiting for Classic in the car, the longer they waited for him, the more he thought of Loose which made him even thirstier to kill Classic.

"Fuck that we going to just light the whole place up, let's put this work in and make a statement on behalf of our boy". Murder spoke out of anger and at that moment he did not care who got hit. He just wanted to retaliate at any one's expense so he can have some type of closure with what happened to his little brother, at least for the mean time.

As Stones emotions was getting the best of him, Classic was walking out the lounge with an entourage following. "We don't have to do all that look", Murder pointed directly at their target. Stone was about to get out of the car and let his gun go off when Murder grabbed his arm and stopped him. "We can't get out the car bro without knowing who's who in that crowd. There are way too many people out here that is linked to Classic. As far as we know they all down with him and are ready to ride for him. Besides by the time you get in the car we will be swizz cheesed up".

Murder was right, there are way too many people out here. Trying something recklessly and expect for all to go well is dumb. Even if they got Classic out in the open and got away. Somebody would see something that can incriminate them in the future. Especially nowadays with all the high tech shit the system got, technology is a mother fucker. Stone did shit to get away not get caught up, killing is an art form for him in which he is good at. The difference is you only get one chance to body something and get it right. If not the next twenty-five years would be spending up the river in some rural town. Keeping some hillbillies employed with correctional jobs guaranteeing that they will not go to the bartering system again. Then have employment for their kids in the future before you even get the chance to come home. Then these crackers have the nerve to treat you like shit when you are confined in prison, these ungrateful mother fuckers!!!!!!! No disrespect to anyone but the truth is the truth!

Murder drove slowly down the street to give them both a better look when they take fire. That's when he and Murder let off countless rounds at the crowd. Without a care of who the bullets hit if it hit something. Stone backed his seat up so that he was able to shoot from the back window while Murder shot from the front passenger side keeping one hand on the steering wheel.

A few bodies dropped instantly, while the rest ran in all directions not ever knowing who the bullets were intended for. They looked like roaches going in all directions when you turn the lights on in a roach infested apartment. In the hood a nigga is not trying to find out who the bullets are for any way. Slugs have no names and they do not discriminate what or who they penetrate.

The messed-up part of it all, Classic went untouched, while it was a few innocent people that got injured by stray bullets. But from all the dirt that his Set did in the hood. No one knew why the assailants did it and for who the shots were intended for. This was just a part of the lifestyle they chose, a sad cycle that will never have an end to it, or at least it seems like that.

"You see them running all scared bro", Murdered said all excited from the adrenaline. "We shot at least five of them bitch ass, hard back, mother fuckers. That's what the fuck I'm talking about, we should go back and hit five more". Murder was always a little on the crazy side, but Stone kept a tight leash on him. Knowing if he did not, he would have ended up dead or in prison a long time ago.

"Who gives a fuck Murder, the only shit I'm trying to hear is that Classic is dead. You got that?" Stone asked him firmly. "So, if ten more people got to get it before he does, let it be. You know how it is, there is never no rules when it comes to love or war. Let's just get some rest tonight for tomorrow is going to be a long day with Looses wake and all". They stopped at the Brooklyn bridge for a second so that he could get rid of the guns by throwing them into the river before disabling them. They made a quick stop and made sure no one would see them toss the hammers. Stone took the guns apart and tossed them piece by piece into the waters.

"Now get us back to the Bronx Murder I'm fucking beat". It's crazy how you get so accustomed to taking lives in the hood. At the end of the day if you want to train an American soldier to not deal with war symptoms let him live in the hood for a little while. Killing people for us is as simple as taking a shower in the morning or better yet brushing our teeth. It's not that we are raised as savages, it's only that from a young age we get accustomed to tragedy.

CHAPTER 7

E very one that knew Loose was at his wake paying him respect. He was much loved by everybody in the hood as if he was family. Stone hated everything about wakes from the smell, the crying, but most of all, the saying goodbye to a love one. This will be the last time he will lay eyes on his boy Loose in the flesh. From here on out he will only live in his heart. Other than that, he will be a memory of the past. His mom was so hurt, Stone wanted to approach her and tell her so much, but he was short on words. He did not want to say anything that will hurt her anymore then she already is. There's nothing that he can tell her that will bring her son back. Stone saw that Cheryl; Loose mom was staring at him from the moment he walked in the door. That made Stone feel awkward to the point he avoided to make eye contact with her.

About an hour later Cheryl approached Stone

gave him a hug then grabbed him by his hand. As she pulled him away from who he was speaking to Cheryl began to speak. "Could you let me speak to you in private Stone?" Even though she asked him politely he knew she was demanding him by the way she was pulling him as she walked away. Once the two were out of hearing range of the others she continued the conversation. "I'm going to get straight to the point with you without holding any punches. Whatever we speak upon will never bring my son back. There is nobody to blame but my son for choosing to live the lifestyle that he lived. He lost his life for it and I know I raised him good enough for him to know what he was doing was not right or safe at all. Now that he is gone, I need something from you. I'm going to ask you to find the bastard that did this to my son and cut his fucking head off". She paused a bit to catch her breath and prevent from crying, "If not I will never forgive you or any of his friends that walked the streets with him. Do you understand?" she asked him but again it was more of a demand to him.

"With all due respect Cheryl in a way I do feel guilty that your son's life was taken by these streets. But I do promise those responsible got it coming to them bad. I will make it rain for forty days and forty nights if I have too. But I will not rest until those responsible have paid in full. I honestly won't think it will take that long but please bear with me, it will be done"!

"That's all I wanted to hear Stone; I was told you are a man of your words. So at least I can sleep at night knowing his killers will pay for what they have done in due time".

Cheryl gave Stone a hug and thanked him ahead of time. "I also want to thank you for the assistance you have given us to make sure I buried my son like a king. There are not too many people nowadays that live by the old code. I give you so much respect Stone, you sure are cut from a different cloth, compared to the people that live that life nowadays".

What Stone saw next really got his blood boiling for he could not believe his eyes. He looked over Cheryl shoulder and saw that Bump was talking to X at Loose's wake. To top it off he came dressed to impress with bright colors not showing respect to his fallen soldier. Then Bump had the nerve to be kicking it with X like if they best friends or something, Stone was not having it! He excused himself from Cheryl to stop the little chit chat they had going. Making sure X and his little team leave with or without altercations.

"Ayo Bump let me talk to you", Stone said with a mad dog face. He paid no mind to X which was hard cause he came in here looking like a celebrity shining with all the jewels he had on. This was not the same X he saw on New Year's Day. It's like the more money they make this lame was getting a share of the takings. That's when it crossed his mind that Bump could be dealing with X. The thought alone gave Stone the urge to kill him on the spot. But his actions were only based on facts not assumptions.

"Let me ask you a question Bump are you dealing with him", pointing at X. "Please let me know I'm bugging Bump, if not you know shit is going to get really ugly, real fast up in this bitch".

"He just came here to pay his respect to Loose and his family". Bump spoke like if Stone feelings didn't matter, as if it was him that was calling the shots. "Don' t bug out over nothing Stone, you make a big deal over matters that you shouldn't. We all deal with hard times but let's not let this hard time make us think or act crazy".

"I'm Loose family and we don't need him to pay respect to Loose. So, do me the favor and tell this buster to get his sorry ass up out of here. If not, more reservations would have to be made at this funeral home in a few days. I'm not taking it lightly at all either Bump". As he spoke his emotions began to get the best of him. "I'm five-seconds from losing my cool up in here my dude," then calmly said "I don' t wants to disrespect Cheryl or Loose. Now if it comes down to that a lot of people will suffer for it".

"So, don't disrespect them up in here then", Bump sound annoyed. "All you got to do is calm down and don't look at his face, act as if he's not up in here".

Stone did everything in his power to not put his hands-on Bump. Stone did a great job at shading those feelings though. "I don't know where you get these new set of balls from Bump. But do me the favor and don't test my patience right now. Its ready to get popping up in here and you going to be the one to blame. Only cause you not telling this man to leave". Stone then changed his mind and decided to do it his self,

"You know what, I got this, I never had a problem doing things myself, you should know that by now Bumpy". There were a few people that saw what was about to go down. So, they quietly got up from their chairs, getting out of harm's way. They knew everyone well and the reputation that followed them. So, the best bet is to not get caught in the middle of these titans colliding.

"You don't have to do that I'll take care of it". Bump then stopped Stone on his tracks by putting his hands on his chest. "I just don't see what the big problem is between the two of you."

One thing was for sure and that is that Stone

does back up what he says. "Let me tell you something else Bump, he better not be getting any money with us. I don't like him, he's a snake in the grass. The best way you take care of slime like him is to not fuck with him at all, is that understood"? Stone grabbed Bump by both arms and was inches from his face as he spoke to him.

Stone spoke of X like he was not there totally ignoring him. He already did all the talking he was going to do with him. That New Year's incident was the last time Stone will talk to him. The funny shit is X just stood there listening without putting his sense in it. X knew he was way out of pocket and out gunned. Stone then let go of Bump and got a good look at the other faces that X was with. Intentionally letting them know that he is getting a good look at them. He only did it to see their reactions so he can see what kind of goons they really are. They all kept there poker faces playing their part to a tee. Letting him know they did not give a fuck and are ready for whatever.

"I got that Stone", Bump then began to speak to X. As Stone walked off, he told X the best thing for him to do is leave. He could not believe Bump. But the seriousness in his face let him know that was the best move for him to make. X knew never to take Stone lightly especially in a time like this. They lost one of their own. So, God knows shit could get crazy. With all the stirred-up emotions one goes through. When losing someone they really love.

"That's cool, I guess I talk to you later" X left the place with his team walking right behind him. He knew the time will soon come where they'll be holding court in these streets. So, to make any kind of drama right now will be childish games. That is the shit only a scare nigga does to blow shit out of proportion. Redrum, X's goon, did not like the way Stone spoke to Bump. He's a violent man that played no games with others and did what he did well. He found any reason to do what he liked best and that's to put that work in. His business was simple it is to serve death to the highest bidder. But being light complexion with hazel eyes and good hair didn't make him look that intimidating. That is the reason in which makes him more dangerous than many. The element of surprise was always an advantage for the one being underestimated or under looked in war.

"What up X let's do that man something ugly right here, right now! I'm not feeling the way he speaks like he can't get it where he stands. You know how I move; I be the one to take him out. It would mean nothing to me to dirt nap him right now."

"Just be easy Red there's time for that later.

Besides this is not the place for it. If it's one thing Red I have respect for the dead. Especially since the dead man moms go back with my mom's for years, how can I do that to her?"

Red looked back to give Stone a mad dog stare in which he made Stone laugh. Stone seen no threat in the man not because he felt he was a lame. Surely by the way he carries himself you could easily see he has a head on his shoulders. Besides, we all know that real recognize real in the jungle. But because he is fucking with X fuck him and die slow too.

"Bump what up with that man, he into face fighting". Stone asked pointing at Red as he walked away and out of view. "You better let him know what time it is with me. As a matter a fact Bump, do me a favor and let me not see you with those lames anymore. Unless you want to stand on the other side of home team. Let me ask you another question, is he getting money with us? Please don't let me find out he is because our friendship is at stake. If you are supplying that lame with our product that will be the end of us".

Bump did not say a word; he just gave Stone a blank look answering Stones question without speaking. Bump was getting tired of not being able to move on his own. He did not know how much longer he will be able to keep doing business with Stone. If he is getting money with Stone, he will forever hang under the wings of him. The only true reason he was still around was because Stone had the connect. If not for that one reason, he would have been turned the corner a long time ago. How you can compete with a man that is hitting everybody off with that fire?

"I'll speak to you later Bump, I got more important business to take care of then be talking about X". Stone got on the phone and decided to get in touch with Santos so they can discuss them Brooklyn cats.

"Hey Santos, what up my brother, how things down there in sunny Miami"?

"Can't complain about a thing just taking it real easy enjoying the day, how about you"? Santos had a beach bunny fresh out of College swallowing him like a pro for a small fee.

"Santos I'm calling only to tell you that I am considering taking you up on the offer you proposed a few months ago. I need to clean a few things up here that needs the services of an outsider."

"Cool, I can start heading towards New York the moment this pretty little mami is finish paying her dues." As he spoke to him on the phone, he lifted the lady's chin so that she can give him eye contact. It thrilled him to see her gagging and tearing from the thorough face fuck he was giving her for a bullshit hundred dollars.

"Good! That means I'll see you real soon because it should not take you no more than a minute to finish what you're doing", Stone joked.

"Fuck you Stone," he then laughed cause Stone was correct about what he just said. As a matter of fact, I will be on my way right now. Santos pushed the girls off his lap and wasted no time to get to the door as he headed to New York. She asked Santos where he was going but he totally ignored the question telling her that she knew her way out. Walking out of the house he tossed a crisp hundred-dollar bill on the floor. He then threw a second bill on the floor, "the extra bill is so you can leave right now." By the time Santos got into his car the young lady started the ignition on her car half dressed. The shit people do for pennies Santos thought to himself as he started his car and drove to the airport.

Stone stood for another half hour by Cheryl side till he decided it was time to get up out of there. At the end of the day he did everything he could do for his comrade. The only thing that's left to do is kill Classic, so that Loose can rest in peace. He had told Loose to tone the flashing down when he was alive, but he did different. He knew if he would have kept things simple he still would have been alive. There's no turning back from death and now he was gone forever.

Stone looked at Cindy and from his stare alone

she knew what he was trying to say. She said her good-byes grabbed China's hand and told her it was time to go. As they walked out of the funeral home China seen that there was a crown Victoria car parked across the street. Off the top she knew it was the homicide police trying to get some leads on Loose's murder. But what really got her feeling a little nervous was that X and his little clique were parked just three cars behind the police car in an all-white Range Rover.

"Cindy why the fuck is X parked so close to the police," China asked. "I know them lames are not giving it up like that. They fucking with the police like that shit is in style or something? Then have the nerve to stay right there with no shame to their game."

"I don't know just don't pay any of them any mind. You know how mother fuckers are nowadays. They act all tough till you rough them up. Then their asses be in the precinct pressing charges acting like fucking victims."

"I don't like this Stone, those lames leave and now the police are out here, what you think about that?"

"I don't know, you think they are going out like that telling on people. I think it's just police doing what they do. Besides I know X is not giving it up like that. Just cause I don't fuck with him stops him from being a real mother fucker."

"I'm telling you them dudes are all rats. There is not a single real bone in them. That will allow it to keep it gangster or hold water when they get caught up."

"You don't have to tell him nothing he sees for himself," Sin told China. "You don't have to worry everybody knows you didn't have anything to do with Loose's death. But now X is becoming a pain in the ass, he's trying to be seen a little too much."

I swear I can't stand that bitch ass nigga X. Out of all the people that get killed, why it couldn't be him? I'm telling you he not going to pass the summer if he keeps it up!"

No one knew the reason why Stone and X didn't get along. But it's because of what X did to Cindy a few years back that Stone feels the way he does about him. Even though he loved her Stone could never picture himself killing for a female. Now killing a person for money was a totally different story for Stone.

As they walked out of the funeral home in the direction of Stones car. The police got out of the Crown Vic and walked towards the trio.

"Excuse me may I have a word with you for a second." An officer known as Watts asked Stone as he started to walk towards him.

"Right now, is not the time officers. I'm not in a mood to speak. But if you can give me your number, I can call you when the time is right." Stone was being polite only because he had his hammer on him in a holster. He did everything in his power to not get searched.

"I don't think that's an option for you," Officer Cruz jumped at Stone to apprehend him. But he just did not have what it takes to do it. Stone two pieced the officer with hooks knocking him out to the point he was in a deep sleep. In two seconds flat the officer was snoring loudly in the middle of the street. He took off running putting his head down not looking back. Watts knew he would not be able to catch up to him. So, he never took a step after him. Stone ran up the block like a track star and turned the corner. It amazed Watts to see a man of his size move so fast.

China could not believe what she just saw. Cindy couldn't stop laughing from what she just saw. Stones big ass taking off the way he did. By the time he took his third step they all knew he was gone, away from police reach. The girls walked towards the car keeping their cool, but it did not stop Cindy from laughing out loud. "Why the fuck you laughing at Cindy, did you not just see those bastards try to grab Stone?"

"Yeah, I saw that, but did you see him knock one of them out? Then see his big ass run like a hundred miles an hour, that was some funny shit." A few minutes later Cindy's phone rang, and it was Stone.

"What's up baby let me know where you at so I

can go pick you up. I'm telling you pappi you are one crazy mother fucker I swear."

Stone laughed, "Nah you don't have to pick me up. I'm in a cab already going to my house just meet me there. I just want to know why homicide police jumped out on me like that. It appeared to me that they are trying to take me in. I cannot understand what that was all about." It puzzled him but one thing was for sure, time tells everything.

"Babes you think X had something to do with it, he was right next to them. You know there is a lot of bitch in him, so at the end of the day we can't put that pass him."

"Like I said before, I don't think it's him. But we talk about that later." Stone hung up the phone not believing that those lames tried to set his ass up. As he was getting home the vision of X appeared in his head again. With all the jewels, a range rover, and top of the line gear, Bump had to be hitting him off. He was convinced and if he could ever prove it Bump ass is out of here. He just couldn't understand Bumps madness he had shit going so good for him. Why would he fuck that up? After all this time Stone has only been a brother to him. So why would he go against the grain and deal with the enemy, Stone thought. I guess it comes down to the same reason why Cane killed Abel.

X did some real foul shit telling the police that he believed the person guilty of murdering Loose was at the wake giving them Stones description. Even though he knew Stone had nothing to do with it. He just wanted police to search him to make sure he was not armed with a burner. That's the oldest trick in the book for a bitch nigga. The moment the pigs search and leave him alone he would have come and light his ass up. His intentions were to kill him right then and there, only because Red got to X's head. Telling him that he must get him there and not wait for another moment. We might not have another chance.

It did not work out like that for them. He now hoped that nobody will find out it was him that had gotten the police on Stone. He knew Stones bitches observed X scheming, so from this moment on he had to be low key. He knows Stone is a heavy hitter that's getting a lot of money and people like that can't be taken lightly. He's bound to send your own people to take your head off for the right price.

His phone ran and it was Bump calling him, "what's popping Bumps."

"Fuck you think, you got to start playing your cards right with Stone. If not, we'll all end up floating somewhere down the Bronx River with bullets wounds to our skulls. I don't know what it is with you X but it's like you got shit to prove to Stone. From now on its strictly business with us, Got that! I'm not going to let your foolishness get me killed or cut off," Bump was highly upset with X.

"It has always been strictly business! What you think that we peoples or something? This game is all about money if not I won't be playing in it. Take my advice though, stop being scared and get yourself a dog." X didn't wait for a response he just hung up the phone on Bump tired of his scared ass.

"Red you believe this scared ass nigga is calling me all worried. That's what happens when you play both sides of the fence. He would of never lose sleep if he had a loyal bone in his body."

"You already know X, I told you from the get. We should put his ass out to avoid future conflict from the jump."

"It's all about timing Red you should know that this is not the eighteen hundreds, where we in the wild-wild west. You go to jail easily for what you do nowadays."

"Shit if you scared get a dog," Red was only joking with X. They broke out laughing,

"Fuck them lets go get some bud, some females, and chill for the rest of the day. I need to get my head right from all the bullshit that is going on right now."

"That sounds like a plan," Red was always ready for a good time only cause he knew his lifestyle will one day come to an end, All GOOD THINGS DO.

Stone always enjoys the sex in which he shares with China. But to be honest he enjoyed Cindy just as much or if not more. At times he asked himself if they would have been the way they are with him if he had no money. The answer will of course be no except for Cindy.

But fuck it cause he do have money and that's that. He had China in the doggie style position slow stroking her while caressing the small of her back. The squeals that came out of her mouth were of a woman having pure pleasure. She loved the spot in which Stone hit when they have sex. She was about to cum when he Stopped cause his phone rang.

"Sorry babes I'm expecting an important phone call. I know how much you hate it when we stop."

"When are your phone calls not important?" China understood it was always business before pleasure but still that did not stop her from getting upset.

"When they not about money babes," Stone answered the phone knowing it was Santos.

"It's me Santos, I'm just calling to tell you I'm in the Marriott. I'm going to get me a good night sleep, so I'll see you tomorrow."

"Then tomorrow it is Santos," Stone hung up then turned his phone off. Knowing Santos was in the city made him feel a lot better. He was tired of all the games that are being played. It was time that bodies start to drop, if not the streets will get braver and more trouble would come their way.

That night he made love to China instead of just sex. Tonight, was different for some reason he wanted more from her; he just did not know what it was.

After his love making Stone looked back at his day and reflected on everything. It gave him the chills when he thought of Bump dealing with X. Could it be that X just wants to get money and that's it? That is something he kept questioning day in day out. Nah, not that nigga, he's never up to no good, but who is in the streets? He tapped China on the shoulder to wake her from her sleep.

"What's up pappi, Are you O.K?" Something must be wrong if he woke her up this late, she thought.

"Yeah I'm good I just want to ask you a question and please be honest."

"Ask me whatever you want babes and don't be stupid you know I will always be honest with you."

"What do you feel about Bump, I mean as far as the way he moves and where do you think his loyalty is at."

"I don't trust him; His loyalty is for himself and I feel he has been like that since the day I met him. I always kept my eye on him, I swear baby don't trust him. You could clearly see that he wants what you have. People like that are only good dead. Unless you have an agenda for him that no one else see."

When China said that he thought of X and Bump. Chills ran up his spine picturing the two plotting on killing him. First, I got to take care of Classic. But I swear to all I love shit is going to get hectic. Classic must go fast he owes Loose and his mother that much.

CHAPTER 8

Murder, Cindy, and Santos waited patiently for Classic to come out of his building. They did not appear much of a threat to anyone. Looking like they were on their way to church is what gave them an advantage. To overlook an opponent is to lose a battle before it starts. That's Santos philosophy on how to plan during an act of war. Who can battle with one they can't see? It's like the way of the ninja, Santos was the king of deception in Miami. That simple reason made him one of the most feared men there. He never missed his target and plans to never miss either. The element of surprise gives everyone the advantage even when under sized or under skilled.

Santos was leaning on the car talking to Cindy but listening to what was going on around him. He knew he had to be really careful with these men not because of their skill at combat. But because they are so many of them and there is always strength in numbers. It's obvious that they are gang bangers and from his knowledge the only way they know how to move in is in packs. You rarely find a lion in a pack of hyenas. But it does not mean the bite won't hurt you.

Santos kept his ear to one specific clown listening to what he had to say. The man could not keep his mouth quiet. What amazed Santos was that the rest listened, hypnotized like he was speaking a gospel. After about twenty minutes of talking Santos picked up that he was Classics' brother. How can a man speak so reckless without knowing who was out there listening? Santos didn't give a fuck to be honest he was glad at his dumb ass. He just made his job a lot easier. He knew then and there who his target was going to be for the day.

"Do me a favor and meet me around the block Murder. Cindy you go with him, I will see you in a couple of minutes."

Murder did what Santos asked of him. On the other hand, Cindy tried to tell Santos not to rush things. Only so that they can do it right.

"With all due respect sweetheart this is what I do. I know when the right time is and when it's not. Now please get in the car and wait patiently with Murder, I should not take long." He gave her a little wink of the eye and rubbed the small of her back.

Cindy could not protest; she was a little nervous as always. But who's not when it comes to times like this? To think that one mistake could cost you your life or a lifetime in prison is nerve wrecking.

"O.K Santos just be careful and don't rush it. These are dirt balls that might never get another shot at money. So, no matter how long this will take they will always be in the hood."

"That may be true but still it has to happen now." Santos opened the passenger car door, grabbed Cindy by the arm very lightly, and guided her into the car. "Don't worry about a thing, I'm going to be extra careful just for you." He then winked at her again which made her blush a little. The funny shit was she did not know why. Murder pulled off and did what was told of him to do.

Santos had a thirty-eight special with two speed loaders. But this was in case of a worst case scenario. His favorite weapon was a switch blade only for its consistency, it was quiet and never ran out of bullets. He could always depend on it without failing him like guns do at times. He looked up and down the block and knew if something was going to go down it had to be now.

Santos walked up on the man and introduced himself in a very timid manner. He walked up on the man giving him the impression that he needed something. But at the same time looking alert of his surroundings.

"Hello there, my name is Miguel and yours", Santos asked then looked around as if he was looking out for police.

Milk did not know what to expect of the man. But by his size he saw no threat in him. If anything, he looked more like a person you can victimize and get away with it.

"My name is Milk," putting his hand out so that Santos can shake. "Nice meeting you. Now tell me what you want because time is money. So that does not give you too much time."

"Oh, with all due respect I am not trying to waste your time. If anything I believe my time will benefit you since your time is money. Especially when they aren't that many hours in the day. To accomplish everything that needs to be done." Santos got Milks attention; you can tell by the way his eyes lit up. They looked like one of a deer in front of head lights. Right before they get smashed on the road by a moving vehicle.

"I was wondering where I can get some merchandise? But it must be good quality at a reasonable price. I'm a big spender and I was told that your prices on blow are fair. I'm trying to get treated good by a connect only because I spend a lot of money, mind you. So, at the end of the day no one will be taking a lost for their time."

You can see the thirst in Milks eyes. "If you don't mind me asking. How much cash are you willing to spend?"

Santos pause for a second and looked up as if he was calculating. "Twenty thousand dollars," Santos did not hesitate one-bit convincing Milk he had the money. By the look Milk gave him, Santos knew he had him on the palm of his hand. The easiest man to get is a greedy one or one in need. There are many traps you can use to bring him in it's ridiculous.

Milk just knew he had an easy come up with this man. He told him he can give him a kilo for that much cash. Just by what Milk told him got Santos very angry. At those prices Santos was not going to get shit but robbed. That meant killing this crook was going to be a lot sweeter for Santos.

Santos tried his best to look happy for the deal he was getting. "That's beautiful Milk, so when can we make the transaction?"

"As soon as you get your bread right, we can go get the product. I have it close by. It will take no more than a minute to get to it. I can't show you nothing until I see the cash though. You know how the game is in these streets. Money on the wood make the game really good."

"The money is around the block; we can go get it right now!" Santos walked towards the corner and Milk followed closely keeping his eyes on the prize. "I got him where I want him" Santos thought to himself. Milk was already distracted thinking of what he was going to get with the money he takes from this man. As he was daydreaming Santos went into his pocket taking out his switch blade. What happened next took Milk by surprise. All he felt was a light blow to his throat. Instantly blood ran down his body warming his chest and stomach area. Santos in one quick motion spun around hitting his neck with the blade. It was so quick that no one saw what the fuck just happened. Doing it in broad day light just made the rush for Santos so much higher.

He slit his throat with all his might to make sure it's a one-shot deal. By the gargling sound that Milk made Santos knew there was no coming back. It was a deep wound that cut his jugular vein clean. Milk grabbed his neck realizing what was happening to him. Terror took over his body knowing that real soon he will meet his maker. He tried to yell out for help, but panic prevented him to do so. His body froze from the horror he was experiencing. Nobody was there to help him in his last moments. The sad part he was only a few yards away from his so-called peoples. "I'm going to die alone on my own block. Having my comrades oblivious to the fact that I am dying right next to them." His last thought was a questioning to God. "Was I that bad that I'm dying here like a dog?" He took his last breath knowing the answer to his question.

"Job well done," Santos credit himself on the work he just put in on Milk. He looked around to make sure there was no witness or wanna be heroes. He walked around the corner then jogged to where Murder was parked. As soon as Santos got in the car Murder looked in his rear-view mirror. When he saw no one was behind Santos or notice him get in the car. He darted out into traffic a little on the fast side.

"Easy man, take your foot off the gas pedal. You driving like you just killed someone! You do not want to give yourself up now do you? Let me find out you a rookie at this?" Santos had a sense of humor only cause he was excited he just killed someone. The feeling he receives from an act of violence is second to none. This has been an addiction that has long been out of control.

Santos always made sense when he spoke about things. All he asks of Murder was to blend in with the traffic. There is no reason to drive reckless, especially in the hood. Unless you want to get pulled over and harassed by the pigs. But in their case, it can get a whole lot worse. Murder blend in with traffic and after a few minutes Sin broke the silence. She turned around and asked Santos what went down and if he saw Classic.

"No, I did not see Classic, but I got his brother. Wearing a big smile, he went into his pocket pulling the bloody blade. "Let's just say that if I had enough time. I would of gave him a Colombian necktie." Cindy could not believe that this man was so calm about things like this. What's ironic to Sin is that he looks as if he just got a hit of his favorite drug. He appeared to be like a junky that just hit his vein. Numb, not a feeling or a worry in the world.

She knew then and there that Stone was dealing with niggas way over his league. He is a mother fucker that she wishes Stone would have never dealt with. She kept her feelings to herself because no matter what she tells him. He was already married to the game and committed to Santos and his friends, Blood in, blood out!

Santos told Murder to take him to his hotel suite in downtown Manhattan. "We are going to relax and have a good time now. But don't worry Stone will be on his way shortly." They got to the penthouse suite and right there out in the open Santos had three bowls. One with coke, another with weed, and the third bowl had different kind of pills looking like a bowl of skittles.

"What the fuck are all these drugs for Santos?" Murder asked shocked.

"They mine it helps me deal with my conscience at night. I have seen and done a lot of things that I am not happy with. In which I am not going to get into details with you. But if you want, help yourself and don't be shy. I'm not going to be in denial either, I love to get high." He then popped a few pills chasing it with a double shot of Hennessy.

"Who gives a shit Santos, we not judging". Murder reached over Santos to grab from the weed bowl. "I'll take some of this green though." Murder grabbed a nice size Bud from the bowl inspecting it. Never seeing so much colors in the weed before. "What the fuck is this," Murder asked with a look of amazement in his face.

"That right there is five hundred dollars an ounce. Smoke it and then you tell me what it is. One joint of that right there and you will be in cloud nine. I guarantee you can't smoke a whole blunt without feeling retarded. Last night a joint had me high for like three hours."

As they were talking they got interrupted by a call from the front desk. "Yes, I'm expecting them, send them on up. That's Stone he is at the front desk coming up. You finish rolling that joint up? I'll bet you that will be the best weed that any of you ever smoked."

Stone walked up in the place like he owned the shit. At least for the moment because it's his money that is paying for Santos stay at this hotel. But that was part of his character any way you put it. He just had to let people know he was someone to look at. Stone walked directly to the weed bowl and grabbed enough to fill the three Dutchess he has. It wasn't until he sat down and began to break the bud down that he really looked at it. "This is some real good shit right here. The shit stay stuck to my fingers. That is how you know the THC levels are high in the weed."

Santos waited for Stone to finish that first blunt before asking him to speak in private. He just wanted to discuss paying arrangements and on how he was going to do things. He told him the details of the day and why he killed that kid. "That was his brother and now I plan to get Classic at his wake. Trust me they will not expect something like that Stone. People like them don't believe beef like this exist in this world."

"Santos you do whatever you want to do. Take care of it in whichever way you want to do it. At the end of the day just name your price. We all know the job you do is not cheap. But then again you know you dealing with bank." He pulled out his hand and shook Santo's making a silent agreement.

As he walked out from the master bedroom. He saw that everyone was in the suite including Bump. As of now Bump is still family cause he has not showed other. The truth of the matter is Stone has nothing but love for him. So, until he does not show something different to Stone. He is going to keep things running the way they are. He just prays the evidence does not present itself. If it ever does, then the consequence will be death. But Stone knew it could go both ways. Bump never hesitated on anything and was always eager to pop first. In simple words, he is smart and dangerous.

But as of right now they are all in a need of a break. "Look we have been under stress times in the last few months. Especially with what happened as of late with the death of Loose. So, what I am trying to say is we need some vacation time. It will be cool to relax a bit and get our thoughts right. I know stress Is a mother fucker that at times clog our thoughts. That shit right there contributes to bad decision making. So, let's agree to go somewhere and take a few days off. I do not know of a better way to clear our minds. I was thinking Puerto Rico but like I said we going to where we all agree." To add a little humor Stone looked at Santos and told him he not going. They all laughed at Santos teasing him.

"That sounds like a hell of a plan Stone," Pretty cut in hype jumping out his seat. "I have not been feeling too happy lately. I need some time out to let some of this tension I have get out of my system. I'm also dying to spend some of the money I have been stacking all this time. Shit, a couple of days off from this no sleep hustle would be good for the body."

They all started to laugh, "He's right what good is all this bread if we can't enjoy any of it" Blast said. "If I was to go today the money, I made would not be worth shit. What good is not enjoying two cents from all this hard work we doing. I haven't done anything I have want to do Stone. I know hard work pays off but sheeesh," wiping sweat off his forehead.

"Do what the fuck you want to do. Just make sure you don't carry more than ten stacks in cash. I say we go to P.R cause we don't need passports. From what I hear it's off the hook."

"I don't care where we go let's just go Stone. I need to relieve some of the anxiety that has been building up." The other reason she wanted to leave is to get away from Santos. He gave her the creeps; Cindy didn't know why but he sure did. As she watched him from the corner of her eye. He was in a daze enjoying his high. But not because of the pills and the hard liquor. But by his latest victim Milk which temporary tamed the beast within.

Stone thought it would be a good idea if Cheryl accompany them to Puerto Rico. She was going through so much pain from her son's death. If anybody needed the time out of reality at this moment, it was her. The very first thing that Pretty, Bump, Blast, and the girls did was go shopping to later on hit the club scenes. Stone fell back to catch up on some needed sleep. (no transition from NY to PR) Cheryl did the same in her room. After taking a power nap Stone got dressed and knocked on Cheryl door. He just wanted to make sure she was good and comfortable. He also went to ask her if she wanted to catch up with the rest at the club.

Cheryl opened the door in her under clothes telling Stone to come in. Stone never realized that she looked that good and was in such shape. He had never looked at her in that way but after opening the door half naked. A lot of thoughts ran through his head. As a man he could not prevent the thought of having sex with her right there and then.

"What's up Stone why you are not with the rest having a ball?" She was an experienced woman and could clearly see he was interested and focus on her body.

"I needed the sleep Cheryl. I did not sleep good in weeks to be honest. The question is why you not out with them enjoying yourself? I mean that's the reason I asked you to come with us. So, you can have a good time and get your mind off things."

"I don't know Stone; I just feel a little embarrassed going clubbing with my sons' friends. I should not be here in this room my son should be here." Thinking of Loose brought tears to her eyes. She misses her son so much and it breaks her heart. The fact that he will be gone forever.

"Look Cheryl I can't compare the love I have for Loose with you. Only a mother knows what the love of a son is. But I knew him very well. Enough to know that he won't want you to suffer. He is not around anymore and there is nothing we can do. I mean he will always be in our hearts. But you also need to move on and that is a fact." Stone gave Cheryl a hug then wiped the tears running down her face. Assuring her that life could only get better from such tragedy.

"Now get dressed so we can all enjoy this vacation. It will not be fair to you if we had all the fun. While you just stay behind all miserable in the hotel room. We came as a family and we are going to party as one."

Cheryl always got along with Stone. He was unselfish and a very good friend to her son. But she never really spoke to him like that before. Now that he was so close to her and she can smell him the effect that she was having was different. She was not looking at him as the same boy that ran with her son since back in the days. The person that stood in front of her was a grown man that turned her on by putting his arms around her. Finally, Cheryl made up her mind and decide to go out. "You know what Stone, let's go out and have a good time."

"Cool, just get your dance on and leave all your problems at home. But I tell you right now, don't expect me to dance tonight."

The environment was off the hook and the people where amazing. You know of top that this was no club in New York City. So many fine women but without their stinking ass attitudes. It has been a little while that Stone dressed to impress or even flossed. He caught the eye of half the place male and female. Damn near blinding the entire spot with all the diamonds his jewelry had. He spotted Pretty at the bar but did not know where the rest where. He walked up on him and Pretty was impressed by his appearance. He let him know by giving Stone the two thumbs up, then a high five.

"Where is the rest of the family at?" Stone asked observing the place.

"They in the V.I.P section drunk as hell. You should see Bump and Blast acting a fool. I don't think they ever got this much attention from woman their entire life." Pretty laughed at his comment cause it was the truth. That is when he recognized it was Cheryl that was standing next to him. He did a double take not believe his eyes. He looked at her up and down admiring the view.

"My God Cheryl you look beautiful. I never knew you had such a body. You knocking half the females in here out the box. You need to know that's how good you look."

"Stop playing with me boy, you only getting me upset. Talking to me all friendly like that. I'm your friends mother never forget that."

Stone turned around and looked in Cheryl's eyes. "There is no reason to get upset at a compliment. He's saying the truth you look good, good enough to eat if I may add."

His words made her blush a little. Pretty saw the effects his words had on her and he blew it up, teasing Cheryl.

"Let me find out you feeling my boy Stone Cheryl. Let me find out you a cougar," mocking her by making big cat noises.

"Come on Pretty how is that going to happen. When that is exactly what he is, a boy. I'm a grown woman in search of a man."

"Look don't put me involved in what you two are

talking about. Let's just go into the V.I.P and enjoy the night. I came here to get all the stress I have out of my system. Instead of talking if I am man enough for you."

Pretty was not lying to Stone when he told them that Blast and Bump were acting a fool. They had no less than seven girls on the dance floor. Doing dance steps that Stone never knew they had in them. Bump must be practicing on his dance moves. He is getting a lot better compared to the last time. The girls did what they always do and that's to keep an eye on the boys. When Stone sat next to Cindy, he saw something different about her. Like if she was in a very relaxed and comfortable place.

"What up with you ma, you good," he asked, observing her movement.

"I'm more than good, I'm on a Molly. Being free from all the stress the hood brings is what's making it all the better."

"Oh, so now you popping a Molly without me, where is mine?"

"We all popped babes, we got a bunch of them, for the supper low price."

"Where they at, I'm down to pop a Molly tonight." He waved to a waitress and ordered a bottle of Hennessey. He then asked her to keep fresh water coming to him. Knowing the drug get you all dehydrated especially when you mix it with liquor.

"Right here Stone," China passed the tic tac case to Stone she had stashed on her breast, there must have been five grams in the case. Stone popped two little pebbles and was going to pass them back to China. That is when Cheryl asked for some molly herself. Stone declined until she let him know they all are here to have a good time. She then snatched the case and took a rock popping it not giving him time to protest.

They all pretty much were having a good time. This was something that they were all in need of. After about an hour from arriving Stone was feeling nice and horny from the effect of the Molly. Shit they all felt the same right about now. Stone went back to his room with China and Sin. He had a quick fuck session with them but for some reason he felt a little guilty. Guilty that he left Cheryl behind in the club alone. He should have waited for everyone to call it the night. Before deciding to go back to his room with the girls. Ah fuck it! they all grown and would call it the night when they are good and ready.

He decided to go to her room to see what she was doing. "I be right back; I'm going to check on what the rest are doing right now. I don't want them to get too crazy out here to the point they get in some trouble."

"Sin tried to tell him that they are o.k. but stop in mid-sentence. Knowing Stone does not like being told other when he is about to do something.

He stopped at Cheryl's room first and after the first knock she opened the door. She was cool with answering the door in only a G-string. Stone froze for a second then stepped in the room. Blocking her and closing the door behind him. Only so that she won't be seen by anybody walking the halls of the hotel.

Cheryl was built like a brick house and looked no more than thirty years of age. That's to show that those long hours in the gym do pay off, her body was flawless! Stone looked at her for a moment without saying a word. For some reason it felt normal to be in her presence. Even with the fact that she was not wearing anything but a G-string. Everything was cool until he began to get an erection. He didn't even try to put shade on it. But the urge to make a move on her took over. He looked into her eyes and kissed her. Wasting no time to feel on her body. She stopped him for a second by backing up. He thought he made a mistake kissing her. Then she told him to let her do everything and just go for the ride.

"Sit back and enjoy the ride. I don't want to hear nothing but moans coming out your mouth. Today you will experience how it feels to fuck a grown woman."

"Yeah right, I never had a female make me moan. I like it though cause it's only made you go hard. As a matter of fact, I am the one that's going to do all the fucking."

"You never fucked a bitch like me Stone, I am into pleasing my men there is no other reason for me to have sex."

Stone knew she was a lady in the streets. But now he is also seeing she is a freak in the bed. Oh, I am going to love this, he thought to himself. As a man that is exactly the way you want your women. She slowly took Stone clothes off and was impressed with his length and girth in his mid-section.

"My God you are healthy Stone. Now I know why they call you Stone," she joked.

"That's only one of the reasons that they call me that sweetheart."

She dropped to her knees and wasted no time to give him head. She was very experienced and in about five minutes had him moaning coming in her mouth. She did not stop until she swallowed the very last drop. The drug kept Stone going so he maintained a hard on. He picked her up and threw her on the bed. He pounded on her pussy till the sun came up. The high took over his body and he was in a zone. To the point he never pulled out of her body when he came. By the end of the session he came in her three times. Never thinking of the consequences of getting Cheryl pregnant due to unprotected sex.

That morning guilt settled in for having sex with his dead friend mother. Cheryl appeared more beautiful than ever as she slept peacefully. The sex they shared was amazing, but the guilt settled in and made him feel like shit. He knew that any way you put it; it was wrong. This is Loose moms you just had sex with.

She got up to see Stone in what appears to be having regrets. You can tell by his body language he was uncomfortable. But no matter how he feels he cannot take back what happened.

"Good morning Stone, is everything O.K? I want you to know that it was me that took advantage of you. At the end of the day I can't feel bad for what we did. So do not sweat it Stone cause it should be me that is supposed to feel guilty. I think what happened between the two of us is a good thing. But whatever you do after today I totally understand. But before you make your mind up please let me get some more of you." She pinned him on the bed getting on top of him in a cowgirl position. The rest from there on out is history between the two of them.

For the rest of their stay they all had a ball. Time could not go any faster for them. In the blink of an eye they were all in the plane coming back to the hood. The three days they all spend there made everyone feel better. Except for Cindy knowing Stone had a fling with Cheryl. It did not matter because what goes around comes around, she thought to herself. She felt so betrayed by his actions and of course was also hurt.

If she did not love him for all that he has done for her. She would have left him a long time ago. She made up her mind that she was going to get back at him. How she gets back at him is something she has to decide.

CHAPTER 9

Santos received a call from Stone while he was across the street from the wake. It was only to tell him he's arrived from his mini vacation. He was glad that he was back quick and fast. At the end of the day he wanted to do his job and get back to Miami. But not before getting paid for the duties he's about to fulfill for Stone.

"Good! Stone right now I'm at work so I'll have to talk to you later."

This was the second day that Classics little brother is being viewed at the wake. Yesterday he never got a chance to try anything. Due to the fact that police were around asking questions. Today nothing is going to stop Santos from getting it done. Stone agreed to pay him two hundred and fifty thousand dollars. The shit that Stone don't know about Santos is. He would have done it for a lot less money. This is his passion, his true love, to go out there and take lives.

But for that much cash he will definitely put a lot more love into it.

He walked into unity funeral home after about forty-five minutes of waiting. Only to make sure the coast was clear from police. The smell of the place brings so many memories to Santos. It quickly reminded him of the only person he ever loved, his mom. She suffered her whole life but loved him unconditionally. No matter how hard times where there was always light at the end of the tunnel. She made sure of that no matter what had to be done.

Santos sat right outside the quarters where Milk was being viewed. He sat patiently knowing Classic will walk out of there any second. The thought of killing Classic alone gave Santos an instant erection. Santos carried two 9mm's that were concealed on shoulder holsters. He also wore a belt that held Six extra clips. The longer he waited the more impatient he got, "Man fuck that shit I can't take it no more."

He walked directly into the room straight to where Classic was sitting. He calmly walked to him till he was able to look him straight in the eyes. When he was close enough to lock eyes. A buzz kicked in for Santos, "I got him". Classic knew this was a hit by the look of the man that was approaching him. He tried to reach for his gun but was to slow for the assailant.

Santos dumped three rounds in his head killing him where he sat. In a split second he was gone moving gracefully out of the place. People yelled and did their best to get the fuck up out of his way. It really does not take much out here to become a victim. The ones living that life and were strapped reached for their weapons. It would have been best if they ran with the crowd. Definitely not knowing they are about to dance with the devil. Santos was a pro at this, a mark smith. Whatever he aims at, he hits with a bullseye. All you heard was a barrage of fire blah, blah, blah, pop, pop, pop, pop, blah, La, La, La, La, La, La, La, La, La, La, La. At the end of this hail of fire four men laid dead. Santos was not one of the unlucky ones. He kept a fast pace running out of the building.

He reloaded quickly and hit an exit door. It seemed like a clear get away, until he was spotted ready to get in his car. He could not waste a second getting in the car and turning the ignition. It would have made him a sitting duck for the goons pursuing him. He knew he did not have the time to drive off safely. He would have chance getting shot in the car. He chose to take off running in an area that he was a total stranger too. An army of gang members from the same set as Classic gave chase. Santos ran as fast as he can to get away. But no matter how hard he ran;

they were gaining on him quickly. He spun around emptying the clip of one gun. That quick Santos took three more people out of their misery.

He was giving it his very best to get away. They were not giving him an inch. They fired as Santos ducked behind a car hitting an innocent bystander. He quickly got up, took aim, fired a few more rounds. Another life was taken by Santos actions. It was like an Indian and Cowboy movie scene in the streets of Brooklyn. He will shoot at them and they will shoot back. To the point in which Santos was getting tired. That is when the reality of getting caught by the police or even killed by them began to kicked in. They chased him for eight blocks when he felt a burning sensation on his right shoulder. The impact sent a current of pain making him drop one of his guns.

He cut into housing project's in a desperate act to get away. He knows that if he does not lose them now. He will either end up dead or if lucky in jail. He ducked behind a tree to take his final stand, then, and there. He prayed to his saint Chango as he took aim. He calmly fired quickly taking them out one by one. Santos did his best to take them all out. Pain kicked in from his wound, but he could not give it much thought. He has to keep firing cause the sirens are getting closer. As he lost hope and knew it was the end of his run. A fully automatic weapon fired behind him taking him completely by surprise.

All he can do was drop to his knees with his eyes close. He was ready to meet his maker that very moment. He knew for sure that fire was directed to him. As he was coming with terms that this is the end. The unexpected happen, someone grabbed him by his arm and told him to follow him. It was a big, black, ugly mother fucker, with a chopper in his hand. Santos thanked God for his luck and went with the 300-pound man. As they ran across the basketball court the oversized man put his pointing finger over his lips. Letting the people that saw it all know what time it was without saying a word. They went to the man apartment when he found out his name was Vegas. He wore a pair of all black Chuck Taylors, a pair of khaki slacks, and a red and black lumber jack with a pair of A1 felony shades. In the crib Santos could not believe that he was saved by this man. You can tell he was banging for real.

"Why did you help me, I mean thank you so much for saving my life." Santos checked his arm and more luck to his side his injury was only a flesh wound. "I tell you Vegas, Chango is definitely on my side. All that gun plays and I only came out with a flesh wound."

"It's nothing, those same people killed most of my comrades out here. We have been going to war for a long time. You know what they say, an enemy of my enemy is my friend. It does not take a scholar to understand."

It made sense why Vegas helped him out. But Santos does not give two fucks why he did it. He did for his cost, at his expense. If he knew a way to get to the BX. He would have left Vegas for dead the moment he turned his back to him. Santos did not know anything about this man. The way Santos see it, Vegas can do more harm than good. For all he knew he was just a potential witness. Not a soul in Brooklyn can know what he did today. It would be only a matter of time before this error would haunt him. Way to many people died at this scene to make any mistakes. Especially the way things are now and days in the streets. Only a few live by the code of silence. The rest have no street ethics. They will run their mouth the first opportunity they can to get released. The fucked-up part of it all, it be these misdemeanor ass niggas.

Santos view total chaos as he looked out the window. The middle of the project was filled with police, people crying, and others being nosy ready to Instagram shit. There were three bodies throughout the projects, dead! Cops asked question to whoever was out there being nosy. Santos began to think and knew it's a matter of time. Before someone would say something and point him out. He has to get up out of here now.

"We need to leave and go to a safe place. People are out there speaking to the pigs. You know you cannot trust people now and days. For some reason when it comes to the code, people catch amnesia."

"I ain't worry about nothing! (shout out French Montana, BX stand up). People know better than to open there mouths out here. We run this shit out here with an iron fist. The repercussions are a lot more severe. Then the benefits they will get from being rat bastards. They won't get anything but problems in this part of town. They know what they get if they open there traps." Santos was not trying to chance the bull shit Vegas was talking. The rest of my life is at stake right now, he told himself.

Santos had one thing in mind and that's to get up out of there ASAP! "Do you have a car Vegas?"

"Of course, I have a car, but you have to be easy right now. Just wait till it dies out a little. I take you wherever you want to go. Look at all those cops out there right now," They looked from Vegas window, observing police running around asking questions to the people being nosy. Reporters where doing the same trying to develop a story for the ten o'clock news. Santos has seen enough; he has to get out of here now.

It got to the point where Santos had to tell him anything. Only so Vegas will want to get him out of enemy grounds safe and sound. "You know what Vegas; I make a deal with you. If you get me to the Bronx right now. I will make sure that you get a kilo of coke. You did save my life, so I am in debt to you. I already have a reward for what you have done for me."

Listening to what Santos told him was music to his ears. He can do a whole lot with a key of that white girl. That would put him on the map for real. A whole hood could eat of that plate. His weight will definitely be up, as well as the homies. "Fuck it, let's get up out of here A.S.A.P. I am going to get you to the Bronx right now. With or without the police out there harassing people. As soon as I change my clothes we out of here." They walked out the building right through the crowd of spectators. Santos calmly walked to Vegas car without anyone noticing them.

They got to the Bronx in no time. The two chilled in a lounge to get food, drinks, and share small talk. It did not take long for Stone to get there and join them. Santos instantly explained how he almost got murdered in Brooklyn. If it wasn't for this man right here, I would be dead. They chatted like old friends as they ate their favorite meals. Santos explained to Stone that he is now in debt to

Vegas. He also told him he wants to compensate him for his brave act.

Before Stone said anything, he drank Pepsi to bring down the food. "That is not a problem Santos, consider it done. I will make sure that he would be well taken care of. But for right now let us enjoy this food and order a couple more drinks. Besides we all must be thankful to be sitting at this table right now."

Vegas could not believe the luck he was receiving today. This morning he had a little over an ounce to keep him above water. But the tables turned for him today. By the end of the day he will be able to hit the hood with work. Shortly after an hour and a few drinks. Stone told Vegas to take him for a drive. That way he can give him what he earned. By saving his friend life and getting him back to the Bronx.

"Let's go!" Stone tapped Vegas on the shoulder, got out the chair, then walked outside not saying much to Santos.

Vegas got up instantly cleaning his hands with a napkin. He then reached over the table to shake Santos hand. "Take good care of yourself little man. I also want to thank you for being so generous." That is what Vegas told Santos before he left. The funny shit was he thanked him not knowing what he was offering him. He really thought well about everything, like they say no good deed should go unnoticed. But the truth of the matter is Santos agenda is the total opposite of how things appear.

Santos did not say anything; he just tilt his head in agreement to what Vegas was saying. Why talk when there is nothing else to say. He knew too much and now he had to go for a never-ending ride. Vegas is the only one that can link Santos to the killing spree. I guess this is why they say see no evil.

Stone did not speak much in the car. They sat quietly in the car listening to music. The only time Stone spoke, was to give Vegas directions. Upon arriving he just had to ask Vegas his reason for helping a total stranger. Truthfully speaking Santos was better off dead to Stone only because he played his part already. By killing those foes Santos was not needed by Stone anymore. Who knows one day the same man that helped him out with an issue? Will later become a problem for him, that's just the way the streets are.

"I just had to hold your friend down. He was going to war with the same people that I am at war with. But that little mother fucker was taking on all of them on his own. Your friend is the real deal I lie to you not!"

"Say no more! Come with me so we could go get that right now." They walked towards a private house on a dead-end street right off of Bronx River avenue. As they walked into a dark house Vegas walked behind Stone. He was daydreaming of what he was going to do with the money he made. Never realizing he was walking into an abandon house. That's when Stone broke the silence getting Vegas out of his thoughts.

"You need to live by one rule in life. That shit will help you outlive this jungle Vegas."

"What you trying to tell me with that?" Stone clearly saw in Vegas face that he did not have a clue of what is going on.

"Trust no one!" Bump came from the shadows and damn near shot Vegas head off with a forty caliber. Vegas body jerked violently as he was fighting for his life. He did his best to take the rapper Fabulous advice from one of his song. one into the two, two into the three then you got to breathe. Vegas life was taken from him only because he saved a man's life. His last thoughts before he went lifeless was "damn these streets are foul." The truth of the matter is these streets are foul and it's to everyone. There is no honor for a good deed or person in the hood. No one cares what you do for them. The moment they can eliminate you they will! It's more profitable and safer for the next man out in the jungle. To get you out of the picture.

CHAPTER 10

X was on top of his game running this shit like clockwork. When it came to the dope game, he had his shit on smash. His flow picked up ever since Bump began to supply him. He was getting all of money in the streets. With the exception of Stone and his team. The only problem now was that Bump will not supply him with the amount of heron that he needs. To keep the streets flooded in his part of town. The rating on it was a nine only cause he put no cut in it. He bagged it up the same way he got it. That is the main reason he sold so much of it. It got to the point where he had a few females bagging up around the clock.

When everything is flowing right for some reason Bump slows it down. At times he slows down the supply to keep everything in order. He refused to let X feel like he had control of things. Everything that he made happen was truly cause Bump supplied him.

He also made sure X knew this. That bull shit has X to the point where he thought of taking Bump out. He always says Bump is scared of Stone. No matter how hard he acts around him. X always showed his cool side to keep getting product from Bump. He is lucky he is not able to get a smoker from somebody else. Otherwise his head would have been put out wherever he stand.

Wicked kept reminding X to stack his bread and take shit easy. Opportunity will come knocking at the door. Now when it does, you will be on top of the game. "There is no money with violence X" even though he did not want to hear it, Wicked told him. They worked way too hard to get to where they were at right now. To let one's emotions or machismo get the best of them destroying everything. Wicked is practically the brains of operations only cause of his quick thinking and common sense. His dedication to the team is what brought the best out of all of them. It was his choice to take care of all the business aspect of it. To supply the streets, drop work off, and collect the money. He also kept the girls in order as far as watching them when they bagged up. Wicked is definitely a player of team no sleep. He also set strategies to make sure each spot picked up. Regardless of the clientele they have already.

Right now, wicked had to see X at his house in

Riverdale, (an upscale part of the Bronx). He had to be the bearer of bad news. He had to tell him that one of the corners has slowed down by forty percent. The worst part of it all is that the customers are complaining about the product.

X threw his cup across the room highly upset. "It can't be! How the fuck they could say that the work is no good? I don't even cut the shit. This is some grade A shit. Every block that I put it on, the people love it. Whoever is playing dirty is gonna get it. I'm going to get to the bottom of it." He knew the only way this can happen. Is if one of his main players was doing the team dirty.

"You right X, I know for a fact you not cutting the dope. But somebody is tampering with the product. I already send a few fiends to go buy a few bags. They all said the same shit, it's no good! I'm telling you X he can't be trusted. We must do something about it now. Eventually he is going to try something else. You know people get all brave hearted until you give them repercussions. He's not giving a fuck what he does to the clientele. We fought for a long time to get this block. So, we have to take care of it now!" He then gave X the details of who was doing it and where he lived.

That is not what X wanted to hear. Wicked told him it was Cash that was doing the flim flam. X didn't deal with much of the street's runners. But he got a quick liking for Cash. Today all that shit goes out the window. His disloyalty is going to take him one place, and that's to the grave. "There was no more to talk about Wicked, I will talk to you later." He commended on his job and let him know the problem will be taken care of.

He walked Wicked out the house and immediately called Red. "I need to see you tonight; you know what it is. We got to do what earn us the big bucks out here."

Red lives for this shit, this is how he stay up, financially. So, he didn't care what had to be done. It is going to get done no matter what.

"What time you need me to be there X?" Red asked excited.

"About ten pm."

"Aight peace X, see you later". Shit got real boring for Red as of late. It's really about time that shit get exciting. The only thing is he does not know. That it's one of his dudes that will be taken out.

Ten sharp Red was at X doorstep. If it's one thing X loves about him. Is that the nigga was always on time? He can count on Red to be on time. Red got straight to the point not wasting a second. He never beat behind the bush about nothing.

"Who is it that we got to lay down. I bet is somebody I'm cool with."

X did not say a word for about a minute. Making sure he chose his words wisely with Red. He wanted him to know first, why Cash had to go. Red saw that X was going to give him an explanation and cut him off.

"Look X get to the point with me. Who is he and I don't want to know why? This is my job and whatever has to get done. Will get done regardless if I know them or not."

X had to explain only because he knew the relationship Red has with Cash. Besides an internal issue like this can blow the entire structure. "Red, you know how these streets are. If you let one get away with doing grimy shit. Others will instantly follow to get extra paper. Please, let's not open a can of worms".

Red looked X straight in the eyes and asked him, "Who is he?"

"It's Cash! He's our man that has been cutting throat. By selling bull shit dope with our Stamps on the bags. He has been doing his own thing affecting all our bread."

"I want you to understand something X. I'm in this game playing to win. Now if a nigga that's cool with me. Is not on the same page as us. What can I say other then, that's on him? The question is where we going to get him at? I know my job X, and this is part of the description. I always knew the day will come, in which I will have to put that work in. On someone in which is cool with me or a man in my circle. But that's what comes with the territory of my position. But that's why I get the big bucks, to deal with my conscience. The only thing I say is I'm doing it fast. To make sure no one else knows about it. Let's just keep it between us and God."

Jessica is a master at seducing her men. She usually picks the hustling type of guy. Getting them to do whatever she wants them too. Only because of the way a drug dealer lifestyle is. They will be here one day and gone the next. Her hustle keeps paper at hand all the time. With all the tricks out there, that love to spend money on Females. She made sure she did the things that kept them coming. By now she had Cash by the tips of her finger. Shit's crazy how sex can blind a man of what is really going on. Women can strip you of your true identity. Making you forget what you really stand for. She kept him satisfied with sex making him feel like the man. In return she kept her palms out receiving more than half the money Cash earned. It got to the point that all he cared about was her feelings. To keep her happy, he had to hustle behind X back. That is what selling all that bad dope was about.

A stupid move on Cash behalf. Never thinking

of the consequences that came with trying to keep a piece of pussy happy. The sad part of it all was that she was not loyal to his dumb ass. Little did he know was that Jessica only fucked him for a paycheck. If money was not the motive between the two. She would have never given him the time and day.

He was lying in bed with Jessica watching a movie. When he got a call from X making him pause the movie. X never contacted him under no circumstances. So, it appeared a little on the shady side. He knew that he did not want any money. The simple fact that it was Wicked that handled business. Whatever he wanted didn't matter too Red. At the end of the day he had to play it cool.

"YO X what's good my g? How is things going for you?" Cash acted pretty good when he spoke to X. He sounded like he was actually happy to hear from him.

"Ain't shit Cash, I'm calling to see if all is good. I haven't seen you around in a little bit. I was just wondering when you going to chill with home team. You can't put all your time to get money. At times you got to have the satisfaction of spending a little paper. With all the bullshit we go through in these streets. It's a blessing to have the pleasure of enjoying good times with your friends."

This phone call did not sound good to Cash. He

was going to do everything in his power to avoid going anywhere. But not making it look like he was giving him the run around. "I'm good, just trying to get my money up in these streets. I don't have no time to hang out or spend unnecessary paper. Shit has gotten real slow out here. The fiends don't want to buy cause police keep locking them up. Them fucking pigs really fucking with our paper".

X knows that everything in which comes out of Cash is straight bullshit. He is not going to lose his cool with him. "You have to take your time out here and be safe. Shit get really hot out here at times. Any way you put it; the money is going to be out here in the streets. But not you if you slip and lose your freedom." X knew the nigga was lying to him. He was parked on Cash block seeing the flow of dope fiends going in and out of the building. He hung up the phone highly upset at Cash lying ass.

"Red I want him dead as soon as possible. He can't be alive doing the shit he is doing to us. I don't care what it takes to get it done, get it done! I can't have no one play with mine out here without suffering my wrath. These funny style mother fuckers out here can't be happy with anything. You put them on then and they still want to bite your hand off."

"Calm down X you getting hyped for nothing. Cash will be dead before our day ends. I'll take care of it; believe me nothing goes unpunished around here. Every man will deal with the consequences of their actions. I don't know why you let little shit get you all rowdy. Just drop me off in Harlem and I'll take care of the rest."

Red went too Harlem to get his road dog Chico. At the end of the day they did not have much in common. But together they got shit done. Red was the brains while Chico was all brawn. He is a maniac that was a little sick in the head. Red looked past his funny ways. Only cause Red knew he could go with him to hell and back. Without the man hesitating or complaining a second of the way. The nigga was bout it at everything he did. Even when it came to taking a shit. If anything, his only down fall is he's too much of a live wire. He never thought about repercussions in which cost him to be raised in prison. He spends more than half his life behind the wall.

Red did a lot of dirt, but it never came from his own beef. It's ironic how people make up their mind to kill others for a living. But that's how it is especially in the hood. The streets are overpopulated with snakes. There is not enough for everyone to eat. So, the weak starve while the strong kill each other. In a way it is like the wild where the lion eats the gazelle. It might appear horrible but in reality, the lion did a favor to the other gazelles. The less gazelle in the

Sahara the more they each must eat. With one less gazelle the rest have a better shot at survival.

Red loves the way Chico maintained his crib. The nigga keep it hooked up and perfectly clean. He sat down on the plush butter soft leather sofa. Before he got straight to business, he rolled a blunt. He smoked on the weed until he felt a buzz then passed it to Chico. He then stared at the ceiling enjoying the high he received from this potent bud.

All this time and Red never looked at the television. When he did that is when he noticed Chico is watching porn. I swear this is a funny mother fucker. All the money this nigga gets and all the bitches he can get. He up in this crib watching a porn video. He was about to tell him about his funny ways. When suddenly Red was out of words. He could not believe his eyes. This nigga Chico was the star in the video having sex with a girl, a young girl at that. The more he watched it the more he understood what he was seeing. The fucked-up shit about it all. Is that it was the daughter of one of his workers. In which he had him watching everything at gun point.

"Chi how the fuck you could do shit like this man. Don't you know the more foul shit you do. The worse you'll leave this world when the time comes."

Chico put a dead serious look then tried to justify the reason why he took the pussy.

"The nigga owe me a lot of money that's why I did what I did. Fuck with my money I fuck with what you love. There is nothing else to talk about, as a matter of fact. If you don't want to watch this shit put my blunt down and get the fuck up out of here. You always act like you better than me, but we make the same type of living."

"Just because we get bread the same way does not mean we are alike, you got that! I will never do some of the shit that you do, especially like this", pointing at the flat screen television. "This shit right here is off the wall. Look at the terror in her eyes she must be no older than."

"Fifteen!" Chi yelled over Red voice saying her age with no shame in his game. If anything, he sounded as if he had some sort of pride to what he did to that young lady.

Red hit the off button turning the television off. Instantly changing the conversation to their boy Cash. "Look this is what has to go down tonight". Explaining the reason of why X made the call. After that he had no other words for Chi. He stopped before they do what they usually do all the time. Argue, as if they are cats and dogs. This is the reason why he spends so much time in prison. Chico never took time out to think things through. How the fuck you could do something like this and keep the proof for all to view. You about the dumbest person I know, Red thought to himself.

Just as quick as they started having their differences they forgot about them. Going back to the Bronx Red and Chi went to Cash block. Red told Chi to go to the store and wait for him there. "Keep an eye open and alert me if anything looks funny. Stay on point and when you see Cash walking towards the car. Follow him right to the car and sit behind him."

Red called Cash and told him that he was outside. "Come downstairs real quick, I have some important business that need handling. It's a good thing Cash cause there is money involved". That was all Cash needed to hear, he got to him in two minutes sharp. He was all excited getting into the car. That's how he gets every time he gets the chance to make an extra dollar. The man was so thirsty about getting paper. That is why he is in the predicament he is in right now. One that he will not get around from, his last mistake. At the end of the day playing with money put him in this position. Money that will stay here, while he goes to the other side to meet his maker.

Red did not say a word sitting there quietly. He then drove up to the store, disgusted by Chico not being on point. When Chico saw that Red was parked on the front of the store. He knew he slipped up and got off point, "FUCK". The moment Chi got in the car Cash knew something was wrong. He sat right behind the passenger seat in the car directly behind Cash. People died when Chico comes around the neighborhood. His conscience was not clear with the shit he has been doing as of late. The moment he seen him he knew what this was all about.

"Where you want me to go with you," Cash asked nervously. "I have things I need to take care off. I want you to know I really can't ride with you." He was starting to give excuses just to get the fuck up out of Chi's way. He thought about running but didn't have it in him to open the car door and run for dear life.

"Shut the fuck up Cash, you not going nowhere. Unless we tell you it's o.k. for you to get the fuck up out of here," Chi told him. "We got a few errands to take care of that's part of our job description. But right now, I want some food. I have not ate all day and I'm fucking starving." Chi looked at Cash and tried to sooth him with giving him a phony smile. "You not going to eat some food and smoke hi grade with us?"

They talked Cash into stepping out for a few. They got food, weed, and chilled around the hood. They drove through the quiet blocks avoiding traffic. Listening to music while burning a few blunts. But once Cash got high, he did what he always did. That's to run his mouth a mile a minute. Red could not take it no more; this was his people's. In which had to go so he wanted to fast and painless.

"Don't you got to go home, come on lets go right now." Red drove him to his crib with the intensions of getting him another time. Cash got out of the car and walked toward his building. When Chi asked if he can go upstairs to use his bathroom. The only thing Red thought about was the video and knew he could not let him go to Cash house. It will get ugly up there and Cash was like a friend to him. Red got along with him so the least he could do is make it quick for him, as a favor.

"Who's in your crib?" Red asked

"Nobody my girl went out for the night, she should be out all night with her friends knowing her."

In that case it was all good to go to his crib. He just did not want to over kill people without pay. Sometimes there will be a witness that has to go. It may be foul but that is the way the game is.

They got to the apartment when the worse case scenario happened for Cash. Jessica and another chick were in the crib looking like they were sexing each other. Chi looked over at Red with a grin on his face. At that moment Chico was happy to be in his position. He walked over to the bathroom and let them all know that he was going to use it. He was in there for about ten minutes. It was not because he was using the restroom all that time. He just knew they will become more relaxed if they saw less of him. That is when he came out the bathroom with his gun gripped.

Cash looked shocked but he knew the reason all this was happening. "The nigga X found out the shit I am doing". He thought to himself. Red was never much of a talker. He just nodded his head giving Chi the approval. Basically, telling him to go ahead and put that work in. The fact that Chico is going to kill him bothered him. He got enraged cause it was not much he could do. His actions created his fate to go out this way. He appeared to be enjoying this moment more than anything. "Do me the favor and pull the trigger Red. Don't let this faggot ass nigga do it. I don't want him to have the satisfaction of killing me".

Chico smiled but not because the heart of this man. The truth of the matter is he was not even thinking of him. His mind was corrupted by the images he drew up in his head. With the things he was going to do to the girls in this apartment. "Oh, don't worry about it, Red is going to take care of you. But I will take care of them two." Pointing at the girls then grabbing his crotch. Chi wasted no time to begin to violate the girls in front of them all. Red saw that he had the same look as the video Then and there he knew this man was not only a killer but a monster. Red was not going to play a part of this.

It must happen now without doing anything extra. He grabbed at his waist took aim and fired. He shot Cash right between the eyes. He then had to pull Chi off Jessica before shooting her in the same spot as Cash. As the other girl pleaded, it went to deaf ears. Red walked up on her and put a slug in her temple. Turning around quick wasting no time to get out of the apartment.

"Why the fuck you did it so fast?" Chi was a little upset because Red took all the fun out of it.

"I came here to take care of my business. Instead you want to take pussy you sick mother fucker." Red didn't say much after that. The urge of spinning around and putting a few rounds in Chico hit him. But at the end of the day he knew Chico is an asset. But the way the streets are everything temporary. So, for now Red will maintain to use him as a henchman.

CHAPTER 11

Stone has been spending a lot of time with Cheryl behind closed doors. Only to keep what they have going on, on the low. He did not want anyone to know what has been going on with the two. They have been spending quality time as of late. He knows what they have going on is not right. At times it messes with the little conscience he does have. He tries to justify to himself that they are only comforting each other. With the loss of Loose, but that is not the case. He really is feeling her style, the way she be on her grown woman shit. She was perfect and he plainly loves to be around her. She's his escape from the madness he lives every day. Today Stone decided to pick her up from her job. To tell her how he truly feels about her. He also wants her to take him a little more serious. Although he is younger, he wanted her to know that he can be on his grown man also. The thing is, he does not know how she feels about him.

No one wants to make a fool out of themselves when it comes to your feelings.

He picked her up at her job in a BMW 745LI. Admiring her as she walked towards his car. The way she dresses to work in her executive clothes is an automatic turn on for him. Her clothes fit perfectly, and her legs are of a person that jogs all the time. In his book he rated her a ten. As a woman she was complete all around. She had a brain, a good career, and to top it off she was a dime at her outer shell. The smile she wore on her face as she walked towards him, let him know she was feeling him also.

"What's the miracle that you came to my job and pick me up Stone? What, you not worried what people have to say about us? I mean", she paused for a split second then continued to speak. "I am a lot older than you Stone. Besides you are the friend of my son that is no longer here. Because he was sent back to the essence. Are you not worried what others will think of you? I bet you they are going to say a whole lot about the two of us."

"I'm not worried about what people have to say. I never did worry too much with the exception of my circle. I just want to make sure what I am doing is not wrong. Especially in the eyes of the only few friends I do have. Now let me ask you, do you think what we are doing is wrong?"

"Come on Stone you know what we are doing is wrong. It's not like we were fucking when my son was alive. But I am a grown woman, and nobody can tell me a thing concerning my decisions in life. So, if you don't want a person to know about us, I respect it. I really don't care though, it's our lives and our choice not anybody else's."

"You are right about what you saying right now. That is why I am here speaking to you. I have been thinking about everything that has been going on in my life. I want to make better choices for me and those around me. I will need the help of someone special that is not in the lifestyle in which I am living. I want that person to be you Cheryl. To show you how serious I am. I want you to take a ride with me and see what I have to offer."

Cheryl took a few minutes thinking off what he just said to her. She knows what she wants with Stone at the end of the day. Then after a moment of silence, she spoke again. But not until she thought it through thoroughly making her decision. "You know what Stone lets go, take me to where you want to take me. But it better not be McDonalds," she joked. Punching him very lightly on his shoulder.

They drove for about two hours without saying much to each other. Only cause they are deep in their own thoughts. They got to Long Island in a secluded area where the view was beautiful. The people from there where of a different class. But most importantly of all, not a soul was thinking about them or knew them. They stopped at a bar ordering a few drinks. They small talked until the liquor got them a little on the tipsy side. She led him to the boardwalk and got a view of the waves. Cheryl grabbed his hand and walked with him to the beach shore. The waves roared but the sound had a soothing effect on him. He once again went into a daze when Cheryl broke the silence.

"So, what you want to speak about Stone? I know you didn't bring me this far to walk side by side with me in total silence."

"I want to speak about you Cheryl." He looked at her, smiled, then caressed her face. "It's so many emotions I'm feeling for you right now. I want to make sure you too have some type of feelings towards me. At the end of the day a man hates making a fool out of himself."

"Stone I'm not going to lie to you, I do like you a lot. But understand we live totally different lives. Do you think our views of what goes on in the hood are the same? I lost my son to the streets that is why I never liked anything about it in fear of what happened to him, will happen. It would kill me to have the streets take somebody I love away from me again." She then hugged him tightly and gave him a soft kiss on the lips.

"Look Cheryl since Puerto Rico my time has been dedicated to the streets and you. Don't get it wrong I only do this cause I'm trying to find a way out. This is my way of trying to get out the struggle. So, I'm not in it for the lifestyle. I am in it so that I can get out! I can't say nothing will happen to me cause tomorrow is not promised Cheryl. But at the end of the day, it's not promised to anyone. All I could tell you is that I will play it real safe from here on out. I also want to tell you the people responsible for your son's death, have paid in full." He then passed her the newspaper clipping he took out of his wallet. It says what was done to those responsible for Loose death.

She looked at the clipping and her emotions got the best of her. Once she read the clippings and knew that many paid for the death of her son. It gave her closure making her feel a lot better. It was not right that other families had to go through what she went through. But at that moment she did not care about anybody else feelings but hers. She was glad that the people responsible for killing her baby are dead. When she spoke to Stone, she spoke softly, and her words came out tenderly. "Thank you so much for giving me peace. Now that I know those bastards are dead, I can move on with my life. It also helps my baby to rest in peace. Knowing they are on the other side with him. He can now handle them from wherever he's at hell or heaven."

Being around Cheryl always gave him a sense of security. He always feels secure around her. To the point that he is able to put down his guard and not feel vulnerable. She made it cool for him to do so. This is the reason he does not care how others will see him as. Showing his emotions is something he never did out in the open. But with her it was different because he knew he could put his guard down. He needed her in his life to bring a calm to his storm. This is one of the main reasons he is speaking today with her. To tell her exactly how he is feeling. It took him a little time to build his courage. But he found it in him to tell her, then, and now.

"I need to get this out of my chess. I need to tell you exactly what I am thinking and feeling. I love being around you all the time. When you not around me I can't stop thinking about you. The time that we spend together is not enough for me. So, whatever it takes I want more of you. Shit, I am willing to make our relationship exclusive. I'm not saying let's get married or anything like that. But I want you to be my corner". He paused for a few seconds to see her reaction. Before she can say a word, Stone pulled her into his body. He gently put his arms around her and whispered into her ears. "I never want to let you go Cheryl."

There was something she had to tell him since her son's death. Although she is burning up inside, she will not say a word. Cheryl can't tell him until the right moment. The moment where she knew she has him where she wants him. Until then she will keep it to herself and not tell a soul. At the moment it was another matter in which they had to discuss. So, she broke the bear hug he had her in. looked into his eyes, smiled, then broke the silence.

"Stone there is something I need for you to know. For one it makes me happy that you feel this way. Only because I'm going to bring you news. But before I tell you, you need to understand. This is going to be a decision I make with you, or without you". She stood quiet looked away then began to speak without the eye contact. "I'm pregnant and I am having a baby, your baby."

Stone registered what she just told him. The problem is he did not know how to react. He was filled with so many mixed emotions. He asked himself so many questions that he almost lost his cool. Is it a good thing? Is it mine? If not, who's is it? If it's mine is, he going to love me? Am I going to be a good father? But with all that ran through his mind at this moment. The only thing that he spoke out was. "What did you just say Cheryl?"

"You know what I said Stone, stop being silly. Please listen to what I have to say. I'm six weeks pregnant Stone and you are going to be the father of this child." As she spoke, she grabbed his hands and passed it over her belly.

What he felt when she told him he is going to become a father was priceless. The sound of it all was music to his ears. Being a father was something he has been wanted. Tears rolled down his face from tears of joy. He hugged her, kissed her, and hugged her some more. "So, what are we going to do?"

"I don't know what you going to do. One thing for sure is that I'm moving out the hood. I am going to start a new life with my baby. I'm not going to let the streets consume this one". She rubbed her belly in a circular motion, as she spoke to Stone. "I have to do a better job in raising this baby. I can't bare the pain of losing another child to these streets". Cheryl felt a little guilt over losing Loose. Deep down inside she feels as if she failed as a mother.

"Don't worry about a thing Cheryl. Everything is going to come out just fine. You also need to know that you did a great job raising your son. You are not to blame for what happened to him. He was given everything that he needed in life. Like me, I decided to go out in the streets and chase a fast living."

"I know I am going to raise this child differently. I can't let him be raised in the hood among animals. I am not making the same mistake again. So, if you don't want a part of this responsibility. I will respect your decision Stone. There will be no hard feelings between us either. If anything, I will thank you for giving me another child. It's a gift for me to have a life to give my all too. But I am telling you right now Stone. I am bringing him up away from all the headaches and street shit. Momma is not going to raise a thug this time around. My child will become somebody in this world instead of a statistic."

"But where are you planning to go? What are you going to do? These are questions we need to really think out thoroughly. Before we decide what, our next step is."

I have not made up my mind on where I am going. I do know for sure that I'm leaving. My mind is made up on the fact, that I am leaving the hood. I'm not going to give it any more thought Stone! Whenever I get the chance I am gone."

"If that is the way you feel Cheryl then there is nothing else to say, say no more. The day is so beautiful, lets enjoy the rest of the day and see what life brings."

They enjoyed the day to the point where they lost track of time. Cheryl has to work in the morning. She kept hinting to him that it was time to start calling it the day. As they were driving back home Stone broke the silence. Asking Cheryl if she wanted to make that move today.

"Come on Stone what we just finished speaking about is very serious. I'm not with the games when I speak of my family and progression Stone." She rolled her eyes and looked out the window angry that Stone was mocking her.

"Since when you ever heard of me being about games Cheryl? Look, you can start a new life today. If that is what you want. But if you choose to do so. You must promise that you can do it with leaving the past alone and everyone in it. There are a lot of jealous people out there that would do anything for a come up. So, if this is what you want. Your wishes can be my command right now".

"That is something that I will have to give a lot of thought. I want to get out and give my child a good life. But not with the cost of becoming a prisoner cause of your madness. Seriously, things don't get done right without planning. Where can we go? What are we going to do? There are lots of questions that need answering and issues that need solving."

"What if I tell you that you won't have to worry.

That we have somewhere to live. That you will fall in love with the house. How about if I tell you, I will provide for our family."

"If that was the case then I'll tell you lets go. Without any hesitations or regrets of what I left behind. My past is full of pain in which today I choose to open a new chapter."

"So, you ready to leave all behind? Start new without having any regrets?" Stone only asked her twice cause he had to make sure she understood. He couldn't have her coming back and forth to the hood. "Just know you can't go to the Bronx when you want too. You know the life in which I live. There is no one that I can trust with my family. So please, give it thought and let me know. Take your time with the decision making. But know you have a way out already."

"Cheryl looked into Stones eyes and saw that he was serious. Although she was flattered by his generosity, she knew this is business only. Stone has it coming and he will never see it. At the moment she just must play the perfect bitch. Until he is blinded, set up for the perfect kill. "Stone what if I'm ready to go now?"

"Then we leave now! Know there will be no reason for you to come back. This is something I seriously need you to understand. Do you think it's even possible for you to leave? Without ever looking back at the past and miss it."

She knew her answer but acted as if she was giving it thought. "Stone I can leave the past and not miss anything about it. The only thing is how I am going to support myself."

"Don't worry about nothing, you will be taken good care of. Trust me you don't need to worry about your financial status."

Stone told her to only get what's of importance in her apartment. But to make sure her items didn't deal with bulk. "Cheryl please leave all your clothes behind do not bring much. When we get settled, we will go shopping for everything that is needed." Cheryl didn't know too much about Stone or the money he was getting. So, to her it was a little too hard to believe what was going on. But she went with the flow of things to not spoil anything. She felt a little skeptical about the whole ordeal. Still she decided to along for the ride. She was an independent woman that could hold her own, but she had to see what he was all about.

They drove quietly for an hour as she dozed off. She just got up an hour later and did not know the area in which they were at. It was the GPS system that let her know they were in Connecticut. The thought of what she was getting into kept crossing her mind. Can she follow through on her plans to kill Stone? Only time will tell if she did. Because there are always consequences to a person's actions.

"Alright we are almost there!" Stone told Cheryl to recline her seat so that she can't see the house coming. "Don't look until I tell you too babes and don't peek either."

"What is the big deal about this Stone? I don't know why you trying to surprise me. I never been told I can't look where I'm going." She was only joking for she loved the fact that he was trying to surprise her with house. Just last night she was stressed the hell out. Wondering what she was going to tell Stone concerning the baby. Now no less than twenty-four hours later. He was taking her to their family home. It was as if her dream came true. With God answering her prayers that fast.

"Don't play with me Cheryl. You are in good hands. Please stop trying to be slick and cover your eyes. I could easily see you love things your way. Sorry to say but not this time." He put his hand over her eyes to make sure she could not see anything.

He brought the kid out of her. But she loves every moment of it. "O.K. Stone I'm not gonna look. But at least hurry up and be fast about it. I can't take the anticipation no longer." She giggled, excited to see what he has to offer.

"I'm going to tell you when we get there. Just be patient, we'll get there real soon. We only have a couple more blocks before we get there."

Upon arriving to the house. Stone removed his hands from Cheryl face. He asked her for eye contact. Stone explained to Cheryl that this was only a piece of property. "It's an empty place without a soul to share it with. Know what I have is not only mine but yours. We can share a good life together. All I put is one condition to you. I ask you to make this place a home. I will be the provider while you be the organizer."

It is love at first sight for Cheryl. The place is absolutely beautiful. She didn't know Stone was getting money to afford such a place. She estimated that this house was easily over a million dollars. She didn't know what to say at the moment. Cheryl absorbed the moment and could not believe she was moving into this house. "It's beautiful Stone my God. Are you sure we will be able to maintain a house this size?"

"Stop being silly and get out the car. So, you can see the rest of the house. Mi casa is your casa Cheryl." There was loud barking and a Mexican woman walked out greeting Stone. It was his maid Thelma which lived there since he purchased the house. Since then she has done an excellent job maintaining it.

"Who is she Stone? Don't tell me we have a maid also cause I know you are not Mexican. Damn boy you doing it like that Stone?" Punching him softly on the arm acting as one of the homies.

"She was needed Cheryl, who else would be able to house sit and watch the dogs?" They walked into the house and Stone was having the time of his life-giving Cheryl a tour of the house. All the ooooh's and aahhhhh's let him know she fell in love with the place at first sight.

"This is too good Stone; I must be dreaming pinch me and bring me back to reality." She spun around with her arms spread wide looking at everything, "This is a dream house Stone!"

"The only dream you having right now is your dream house other than that this is real live shit." Out of nowhere came his two Mastiffs looking like colossal pit bulls. "These are my only friends Cheryl that I know will be loyal to the end no matter what. They will love me no matter what, rich or poor, healthy or sick." She did not hear a word he said for she was terrified of the two amazons that stood inches away from her. "Don't worry they won't bite unless I tell them too. So, stop being scared unless you want those two to be dominant over you."

"Let's go to the backyard so you can see the pool." They went to the back and the pool was amazingly huge. The water was so blue, it had a Jacuzzi, a water-fall, even a bar stance inside the pool.

"I do not want to sound nosy but how did you get such a place? I never knew the streets had so much money to let you live like this."

"You don't have to ask questions then, just know everything is paid for and as long as we keep a low-profile people will be out of our business." She seen in his eyes that it will be better for the both that it stays like that. They say that curiosity killed the cat but where he got the money to live like this is something that she will continuously ask herself. She knew he will never tell her so she made an oath to herself that she will never ask him again. The truth is, the less she knows the better cause if the day comes where he has to pay the piper, she will have no knowledge of his activities.

"Get comfortable Cheryl take your shoes off and kick your feet back, this is your house! Give me a minute I will be back I have to get something." Stone excused his self for a moment and when he came back, he handed her a nice mitt of hundreds, fifty grand to be exact.

She was clueless of why he was handing her that amount of money. "What is this for? I'm not going to do anything illegal so please don't even try it."

"Take it easy Cheryl I wouldn't want you to do

something that I would not do myself. I would never consider bringing you into my kind of line. This is so that you can hook the house up to your liking and go shopping for a new wardrobe. If you need anything else don't be afraid to ask. Cheryl understand that in order for me to take care of business. I need to be around the hood, otherwise I can't protect my investments."

She knew there was going to be a catch to it all. "You telling me that to tell me what?" She crossed her arm on defense mode.

"To tell you that for the mean time, I will not be around that much. There is one more thing I need to show you. Come on but you have to close your eyes babes." Stone took her by her hands and walked her to the garage. "Open your hand without opening your eyes, I mean it." Stone place a set of keys on her hands then told her it was cool to open her eyes. When she opened her eyes, she almost past out. He just handed her the keys to a crispy cherry red CLK Mercedes Benz.

That night they had sex like it was their first time ever. As for Cheryl it has been a long time since she had sex the way she was getting it that night. Stone tasted every part of her, then caressed her body, she was sore from the steady pounding she received, his stamina was up to par. It was as if he worked out with the energizer bunny. She begged him to take a break, but it went to deaf ears. He no longer cared about being careful, for she was already pregnant. He went crazy on Cheryl she yelled out of pleasure and pain and could be heard by the neighbors; boy was she a yeller. That night they experienced every sexual position imaginable to them.

The next morning when Stone woke up and had Cheryl in her arms the only excuse, he could give his self was that she is having his seed. He knew it was not right but still going against his ethics. That was some bull shit he was on and he knows that, Getting Loose moms pregnant was some real grimy shit. He did not expect the team to understand so he chose to keep her at a distance from now on. What they don't know won't hurt them that's for sure. He just had to make sure that was the way it stood.

CHAPTER 12

X went through the aggravating procedure that one must go through every time one wants to see a love one in the penal system. This was a bi-monthly procedure that he did for the last two years. He has grown very tired of it and can't wait for his ass to get home already. It is as if they put love ones through so much shit so that it would break family ties and they can return.

Like always he went in there like he owned the place greeting everybody like he knew them in the streets. The thing is there are only a few that keep it tight with those locked up making sure the prison is loaded with escapes through narcotics. With what he did he earned the respect of most of the prisoners. "What's good family? How is life treating you in the belly my brother? I hope nobody tried to take your commissary since the last time I saw you!" X was only joking because he knew his older cousin was nothing to play with.

"The same as the last time you came up to see me. Shit don't change to much up in here until my release date." It's sad for those that are never going home. They're fucked and must stay patient until God calls for them. "You know how I do my G? There is a few things I do but playing soft is definitely not one of them. I just got to get the fuck up out of here. It seems like the shorter you get the more shit come at you and the slower the times gets. It's like the miserable mother fuckers want you to catch a new one or fuck your date up cause you got a shot at society."

"Don't let nobody take you out of your shell Man. Just take it easy cause there's a lot of money out there for the taking. To be honest you shouldn't be stressing your ass got another shot at life. Remember you came up with the bonus then gave them back fifteen plus the life. The good thing is when you get out you not going to have those parole people harassing and knocking on your door in the middle of the night. So, count your blessings, stop crying, and do the last of this fucking time like a man."

"That is the only way I know how to be, A fucking man!" Chew got a reversal from a twenty-five to life sentence to a five to ten but since his disciplinary record was so extensive, he ended up being hit at the board until his max date in a few months.

"So, what's popping with you cuzzo, I hear you doing it real big back home?"

X never got into details with his older cousin so that the street life won't get him all stressed out. There are people that lose all the hair on their head. Being all stressed out from having their mind on the streets. They never spoke about money, bitches, clubs, or what's going on out there in the hood. He just came up visit him, play cards, joke on other prisoners and the overweight guards, reminisce about the past, and when the guards where not looking pass him whatever drugs he can pass him. Usually it was a stick of dope and about a half an ounce of that loud.

"I know we keep shit simple during our visits, but I am going to hit the streets soon. My mind has been focus outside these walls and I want to know what you do so that I could set my mind on what I am getting into once I hit the streets."

"Come on Chuck, you shouldn't think outside these walls until you are finally outside of them. But since you want to know I do the same shit you do in here. Sell that dog food with the exception that you do not get any pussy. X saw that he had the opportunity to hand off the heroin to Chuck. When Chuck got it, he wasted no time to put it away.

They had small talk about the streets and X also put him on to Stone. Chuck was a stick-up kid at heart and nobody knows he's coming home. He also had an itchy finger with a high body count. "Bro I got a crazy come up for when you come home. I'm talking about, this is the only dirt that we have to do and be good for real."

"Word what is it? You know I been lock down for a long-time shit got to be worth it."

"Oh, it's worth it! I'm telling you he got it for days. His team is hitting everybody off with Coke and Dope. I'm getting weight from them, but it's limited right now. Only because they got other people that are closer to them than me." X did not want to tell him the truth about Stones feelings towards him, but he had to draw a picture for Chuck so that he can catch interest on getting him.

The officer called Chuck's government name and told him he had another visitor. "Do you want to refuse or except it?" Chuck looked at the guard in a what are you stupid face. It was a female he met in a festival. She was the wife of an inmate that owed Chuck a little too much money so before he put some steel in him, they made other arrangements. Once at the festival he introduced his wife to Chuck and convinced her to have sex with him in order to save him from a lot of problems. She did her husband the favor but then there was a problem. She fell in love with the way he fucked the dog shit out of her.

Lisa was a dime that always got committed to the wrong guys by choice, so she says. She's a show-stopper at least in the visits! It was clear to everyone there that she worked on seducing as many people as possible. Other inmates and convicts stop there conversations with their visitors to get a look at her when she walks in the visiting floor. She stood about five three which made her look so much thicker. X couldn't believe how Chuck came off with such a dime in jail.

Chuck introduced the two but for some reason X could not get his eyes of her or from the grip he had on her hand.

"Damn cousin you looking at her like you want to eat her right on the spot. Don't mind him Lisa the man doesn't know when he's being a dog."

"It's alright baby, I'm used to people looking at me all the time like that. I can't help it that I'm beau-tiful." She winked her eye at X and blew him a kiss. It was just in her nature to be such a flirt.

"Thank you, Lisa cause Chuck is always trying to blow me, up like if what I do is wrong. It's basically manly instincts since he be around all these cock and balls. My cousin forget what it takes to get his game on. Explain to him that what I do is not wrong."

"It's not wrong but it makes me uncomfortable just a little bit. But I guess it's in a dogs', I mean, in men and their nature to be aggressive." Lisa said it to be funny and sarcastic at the same time.

"Oh, it's like that Lisa, men are dogs? Let me ask you a question, you think all men are dogs?"

"Not all men are dog X," she had to turn her attention to Chuck. "So how has it been baby? Nobody is messing with you. I don't have to call the warden, or anything do I?"

Chuck gave them both a disgusted look, it always gets him upset when a person asks him a question, they already know the answer too. But then smiled and told her that he hasn't been picked on as of late. He had to keep his cool with her and prevent her from seeing his alter ego. She was beautiful but for some reason he wasn't that into her. It wasn't about her appearance, but he was into woman that made it an obstacle to give him the pussy. The way he met her and what she did just wasn't going to make her one of his favorites. To be honest that was what was going to put her on his shit list. He knew in his heart already that the moment he got home he was going to cut her off like a bad habit.

"So, what is up with your husband? Has he been calling you as of late Lisa?" The man felt a certain way and always kept face fighting, so I had to send him, up out of here leaking. I didn't want to, but his funny style ass had to get it. No bullshit! I don't know how his as survive all those stab wounds. I'm just glad his ass didn't die, but I give him his props because he held water and didn't drop dime on me."

"Well he has called me a few more times and told me he was going to kill me for being a disloyal cunt. Fuck him though he will not see the streets in another seventeen years and that is if he behaves. But what I don't understand is why he's mad. In reality he tried to pimp me to you. That shit made me realize he haves no love for me. So, I guess he got what he deserved at the end of the day."

"Just make the right choice Lisa, you know I have no time for a relationship. Being in here all these years is crazy, I just want to go home and take things slow."

"How many times you going to keep saying that Chuck I swear you so repetitive at times. I'm only doing it cause I want to hold you down. All men in this situation that are real men should have a woman like me hold them down. It's just the way shit should be in this world. She felt a little hurt and hoped that none of them saw that she felt a little stupid for getting treated like that by Chuck."

X clearly saw the pain in her eyes no matter how hard she tried to cover her pain. "Don't worry Lisa you'll find somebody out there that would give you the world for the good heart you have."

"Don't get me wrong I fucks with her cuzzo!

When I go home, I'm going to live with her and try to make it work. Do for her as she has been doing for me, hold her down until I get out there! I like her but she understands I have to get my shit in order. That is the only way to you could keep a girl happy. Lisa can you get us some sodas please, from the vending machine, I'm type thirsty." X only asked cause he wanted to speak to Chuck in private.

"Is that all you want X? How about you Chuck, do you want something else besides the soda?" She got up to get them there items from the vending machine but was very curious of what they were speaking about in private.

X being the horn dog that he is had to ask the million-dollar question. "Chuck would you get mad if I try to get some pussy from Lisa?"

"I swear to everything that is the only thing you think about. I already knew you was going to ask me that by the way you looked at her. Whatever you do make sure she keep coming up here to see me and plays her position. Change the subject she coming this way, just do what you got to do and don't get in between me and her."

Lisa walked towards the table and felt a little awkward going to it. She felt like they were talking about her by their body language. "Fuck them!" She only did what she had to do cause things always worked out for her benefit. She gave them each what they asked for, sat down, and acted as if nothing was bothering her.

Chuck gave her an excuse of how he was not feeling well. He then told her she could let X take her back to Harlem. Instead of waiting for the bus to come in a couple of hours. That is where she told him she was staying at right now but is originally from Jamaica, Queens.

"But I just got here not too long-ago Chuck. How you not going to stay till the visit is over when I took this long ass ride? That's foul Chuck you know it takes an entire day for me to just see you for a few hours. I'm going to be honest with you I am upset!"

"Look let us not get into all that right now, my cousin is going to make sure you get home. So, you don't have to wait for that stinking ass bus. If I don't feel well then I just don't feel well!"

She was upset but did not protest because she knew his mind was already made up.

"Come on ma we going to get up out of here in style. Chuck I'm up out of here check you in two weeks. But for the mean time do what you do and stay sucker free. You know us real niggas are a dying breed so we must keep it real with each other. Plus, don't forget stay out of the jail politics! That shit don't pertain to you any more cause real soon you going to be a free man."

Lisa gave Chuck a big hug, a quick kiss then told him she will be there next week. She was upset at the fact that he dismissed her so fast. But the day has not ended, it might not be a total waste after all.

X and Lisa spoke the minimum as they got out of the jail. They really didn't say anything until they walked up to his car.

When she saw what he was driving in, is what gave them a topic to start conversation. "This is a fly ass car X you put up a lot of money to get this hooked up." X had customized everything on it, so it did cost a little money. She still didn't get in the inside to really know how much extra paper he used to hook up the Range the way he wanted it. It was one thing that was certain this man is getting a lot of money. What he was hustling was for her to find out. It's basically her duty to find out what he does to get the paper he getting.

"Thank you, ma, but the truth of it all is that this car is not too expensive compare to what I'm trying to get out of the dealership real soon." They got into the ride, X being the showboat that he is went under the driver's seat and got his jewels. No bull it must have been at least a hundred thousand in jewelry. He then went into the ashtray and got a case filled with small pills. X popped three of them in his mouth then let her know what it was. "Those are X's I like to roll when I'm on the road for long distances. Not to be disrespectful, but you can have one if you like."

She never did drugs in her life but knew she will get better acquainted with him if she was into the things he like, fuck it she told herself. "Why not X I'll take one of those pills it's not like it's going to make me go crazy or anything like that, right? She was a little nervous only cause she heard of its addiction.

"Not at all, the worst thing that could happen is that you might like the high and want a few more pills. Other than that the only thing it do is makes you feel sexy and horny!" He handed her the pill and instructed her to let it dissolve a little in her mouth before swallowing it.

They shared a good conversation on their way back to the city. X liked this girl; she was so down to earth and could relate to what he had to say. As they spoke his mind thought of how it would be like to be in a relationship. One thing for sure though if he was going to be in one, he would want it to be a with girl like this, hood, and beautiful.

Lisa in no time felt the effects in which the drug has. Her pussy was wet and throbbing from the little vibrations the car made driving at 89 miles an hour. There was one thing in her mind for sure and that was sex. She wanted it right at that moment only cause of the drugs affect. She didn't care how she sounded to him she was going to let him know just that. Even if he felt by doing so, she was some kind of smut. "X this shit got me all horny I want to get fucked!" She could of not be more straight forward then she just was.

X couldn't believe that she just said those words to him. Her being that forward made him like her a lot more. "Come on then let's find a hotel close by so I can take care of your itch." He went to his navigation system and punched in nearest hotel. When done he opened his fly pulled out his dick and told her to suck his dick. It was more like an order but one that she was more than happy to comply with. At the end of the day she was used to orders any way.

CHAPTER 14

Stone was exhausted from counting money throughout the night, till daybreak. He was glad to be on the last stack of cash. "Finally, I'm done for the mean time." He kept a down low apartment to stash paper without a soul knowing. Except for the three pit bulls he kept there trained in Siberia to tear up whatever comes up in their space. He even had their voice boxes removed; so, they can be that more silent and deadlier. He lit up a blunt of OG Kush and went into deep thought as he smoked. But was quickly knocked back to reality when he got interrupted by a call from Bump.

At first, he was not going to pick up the phone. But even with him acting funny with him, Bump was still his dog. "What's popping home team how are things going for you? It wouldn't be right, if it wasn't nothing other than great can you say?"

"Well you already know how we do bro; shit is

real good right now. I'm just hollering at you because I am planning to go out tonight." That is there code name when they are speaking about heroin.

"Cool Bump, but you have to give me a little while, cause my hands are tied up for the next hour or so."

Bump hated to wait for Stone but there was nothing he could really do about it, so he went with the flow. "No problem Stone take your time I'll be here in the crib. I wanted to smoke a blunt and chill for a while anyway".

Stone left his crib and walked down the block to his house. Cheryl has made a home of this place to the point where he can have total peace considering all the drama, he lives in. Her belly was beginning to show now, even with the extra weight she carried she still was gorgeous. All he thought about was the child that will soon be in this world that will be his. Lots of thoughts ran in his mind of how it will be with them. He questioned his self as far as, will I be a good father, will this baby love me? He then begged God to bless his son with health, Then the final questioned that always haunted him, will my child pay for all that I have done? Whatever happens in his child life he knew he will do everything in his power to make it better, no matter what it takes!

Stone got to the hood in average time growing

tired of the trips and the game. It got boring for Stone nothing was fun no more even with all the money he has. It became a sick business that your own peoples can't be trusted with the money or the opportunity of power. Even those that come out of the same sand box you must watch and question.

Stone had to go to the other stash house and pick up two hundred fingers of heroin for Bump. He called Bump to let him know he will be around his way in forty-five minutes. Before hanging up he received a call from China and immediately took the call. It was a surprise for Stone cause usually they get in touch whenever he decides to call her.

China has gotten very attached to Stone and since he has not been around lately, she missed him dearly. The game was not fun for her either and she wanted out. She constantly thought about what else is out there for her and what else life has to offer. She knows she has what it takes to make it in corporate America. She has the capital to do whatever she want as far as opening her own business. But in order for her to be happy she knew she had to be with someone sharing her dream. Before she could even say much Stone cut her short letting her know he is in the process of handling business.

He got all the heron, put them in a gift box, wrapped it up, then grabbed a birthday balloon and was out the door when an inner voice told him to stay home. He stopped for a second, then brushed it off telling his self he was bugging out over nothing. He ignored his vibe and went out to check Bump. As of late he has been feeling paranoid over everything, so he thought nothing of it.

As he pulled out of the driveway and turned the block he was pulled over by police. When he saw the lights flashing, he was ready to try them faggots out. The only reason he did not step on the gas was he knew his license was clean and they had no right to search his car. They ran up on him as if they knew he was dirty. He kept his composure and stood cool knowing that they did not have anything on him.

"What is the matter with you officers is everything good with ya?" He spoke calmly and was cocky about the entire situation, for one he knew they had no probable cause but second, he knew he had the financial support to get the best lawyers to eat damn near any case up.

One of the officers instantly curse him out calling him all type of names. Only cause jake hate when you look into their eyes fearlessly. They asked him for his license and registration and told him to wait patiently. They took no more than five minutes to give him back his documentations and told him to have a nice day. The only thing that got him off guard with the entire situation was that they said his name. They did not call him by his government name but by his alias, Stone!

It shocked him to know that the police knew his name. How the fuck these pigs knew my name, Stone questioned. Somebody got to be telling on me, but who? He tried to play it off like he did not know what they were talking about. "What was it that you just called me officer?" doing his best to play it off.

The shorter officer of the two said something but Stone did not hear cause he already pulled off. He looked through his rear-view mirror and when he saw that he was no longer on their radar he sped off. He took the long way to make sure he was not being followed. When he made sure there was no tailgaters he went towards his destination. That's when he received another call from China.

"Hey baby when am I going to get the chance to see you? It's been a long time since I got to spend quality time with you."

"Come on ma you know I've been busy, it's not like I am not fucking with you no more."

"I'm just sick as of late worrying about you. Stone let's leave the game. Drop what you are doing and let's get up out of here." She then started crying saying "I miss you Stone, you should of not trust them, I wanted to be your ride or die."

She lost Stone for he did not know what she was talking to him about. So, he questioned her and what she said next made him hang up the phone.

"You let them kill you Stone" then she stops talking and started weeping. "They killed you baby you shouldn't have trusted them I told you about them."

"This girl is bugging out ". Stone hung the phone up on China.

As he drove the car, he got all paranoid again and his gut feeling was telling him to go home. Once again he ignored all signs and went to go get this money. Stone was all business twenty-four hours a day through rain, sleet, or snow. He stopped at a light when someone called out his name. He looked around but the streets looked deserted, not a soul in sight. Stone being in a rush paid it no mind nor found it weird that there was no one out there. He got so consumed by the game that it got to the point where hearing voices was the norm.

He arrived at Bump house in twenty minutes sharp when he told him forty-five. It was a quiet day today, especially on this block. For being a Friday, there was nobody out there. When he got to the door, to his surprise the door was unlock. That was a first especially for Bump paranoid ass. If it was up to him, he builds a wall where the door supposed to be. Stone walked inside the house and did not see anyone there. He called out for Bump but there was no one or no answer. He then heard what was to him a sign of distress. It was obvious to him that someone was yelling for help in a muffled voice.

He ran up the stairs in the direction of the person yelling. He thought Bump needed him but then stop on his tracks when he saw who it was. Cindy was hogged tied on the floor and Stone clearly saw that she was roughed up.

She got to warn him, not by what she said to him. The look in her eyes is what let Stone know someone was behind him. He spun around but it was too late. A fully automatic weapon rang loudly with Stone as the target. Stone hit the floor hard, knowing he is critically hurt. He did everything in his power to make sure he got to see who the assailant is.

He could not believe he let himself get caught up by him. "How the fuck you know I was coming; Did Bump have anything to do with this?"

X laughed out loud mimicking the joker before speaking. Still he did not say much.

"Of course, he did!" He then walked to over to Cindy standing over her. Releasing to rounds into her head killing her instantly.

"NO!!!" Stone yelled at the top of his lungs, not believing their fate. This couldn't be happening to them like this for they always played the game fair. Looking at Cindy shake like a fish out of water broke his heart.

Bump then walked into the room, pointing his gun at Stone, telling him it's his time now. He then put one slug in Stones head sending him into total darkness.

I guess his inner self was still ticking cause Stone was highly upset for letting his own people take him out. All of a sudden there was a light, then there was an image in the light. As he looked thoroughly squinting his eyes to see what it was, he noticed who it was, it was his boy Loose.

"Stone you going to be good don't worry just do me a favor please." That's when Loose pinched him and Stone woke up in a heavy sweat. The dream felt so real, everything about it. He got up breathing heavy, still feeling Cindy loss. You never know how much you love a person until they not there.

Cheryl comforted him putting her arms around him knowing he is having a bad dream. "Don't worry baby everything is alright now; it is just a dream."

"I know but it felt so real I swear." He told her his dream detail for detail or at least how he remembered. She sat there quietly absorbing every word picturing his dream. Focused on every detail trying her best to not miss a beat. She listened patiently to Stone until he ran out of words. Then she got straight to the point.

"Well I'm going to tell you now, I never trusted Bump!"

"Why you say that Cheryl?" He was interested in her feedback knowing it is easier to see from outside the box.

"Come on Stone, I don't have to tell you that he wants what you have. It's obvious to everyone that he feels like that about you. I guess the rest know you and how you give it up to say a word. I tell you this much, I will never give a person the satisfaction of putting another finger on me. The only way I can guarantee that is to not let anyone know my movement." She got sensitive for a bit but was able to control her emotions. She misses her son Loose so much; it has nothing to do with Stone or his safety. "You know what baby I know a person that is really good with interpreting dreams. I'm going to call him in the morning and make an appointment with him."

Stone was done talking about the dream. So, he reassured her he was fine and to go back to bed. For the rest of the night they laid there deep in their own thoughts. Stone trying to decipher the dream and Cheryl contemplating on how everybody could pay for the death of her son.

After about an hour of tossing and turning on the bed. Stone wait no more and called Cindy to see how she was doing. To his surprise she picked up after a few rings' half a sleep.

"Hey baby I was here half-asleep thinking of you.

Is everything cool with you at your end of the line? I mean I'm not used to getting a call from you in the middle of the night like this."

"You right about that I just wanted to hear your voice."

"That's so sweet babes, I miss you so much when can we spend some time together?"

"We talk about that tomorrow Cindy, I just wanted to hear your voice. Talk to you in the morning sweetheart and get yourself some rest."

"O.K Baby I guess I talk to you in the morning. Love you and be careful," the line then went dead on Stones end.

"Who was that on the phone this late at night," China asked.

"Oh, that was Stone, he said he just wanted to hear my voice and then hung the phone up."

China let her guards down with Stone and had fallen deeply in love with him. She felt jealous that he gives all his attention to Cindy, the game, or and Looses' mother. He thinks nobody knows about him and Cheryl. He not in the hood like that to know what the word on the street is. Plus, everybody getting money to let something like that ruin a good business relationship.

There is so much she must tell him about what is going on with her. There will come the time when she will not be able to hide her pregnancy. She knows time is running out if she wants to be the first to tell him. The only reason she did not tell him anything yet is because she is going to wait until it's too late to get an abortion. She is determined to have Stone baby regardless what people have to say.

The next morning Cheryl and Stone visited a spiritual adviser which is a friend of her family. Friend or not Stone knew for sure this is a hustle. Stone walked into the little store front not impressed with its appearance. He locked eyes with Stone for a split second and knew that everything around Stone was dark. He is not a good person having many suffer behind his actions. Antonio was not in business to tell Stone who he is. He is in it to tell him what he wants to know. So, before anything, business is what bring the two together not common likes.

Antonio shared small talk with Cheryl, then walked with Stone to a room in the back. Where he did his routine and instantly got in his zone. This was just another way for someone to get a hustle on, Stone thought. Even if it was just a hustle, he knew he had to respect everyone's form of living.

"So, Stone why don't you tell me about your dream?"

Stone talked slowly and gave him all the details

of the dream. Once again doing his best to not miss any details. The truth of the matter was even though he did not believe in these types of things. He needed answers for the mind twisting dream he had. So, if it means paying someone a few dollars to tell him about his dream. Then let it be cause right about now he needed answers.

"Well Stone, what is your relationship with all these people?" He asked stone the question while studying him thoroughly. There is a lot that one can pick up from a person's body language.

Stone also spoke with Antonio about his everyday activity. Leaving out at what scale he is doing his thing. Other than that he kept it straight forward with him. Letting him know how he felt about everyone including the girls and X.

"Well Stone I'm going to be honest with you. You need to be very careful with the things you do and the people you surround yourself with. Things don't look good for you, if you stay on this path. I don't have to tell you what the outcome will be. You already know what this lifestyle consists of and its consequences. Now without a doubt there are people out there that want to get you. Will the opportunity present itself Stone, that is all on you? I just advise you to watch those you conduct business with. Those close to you is who can hurt you most. I'm telling you there is always great consequences when the Judas of your circle moves on you. Trust your-self young man and go with your instincts. Who that person is I can't tell you exactly"?

"What about Cindy is she going to be alright out in these streets? I know she will never betray me; I don't care what anybody says".

"Well you know whole heartedly she will never back stab you. But unlucky for her the loyalty she has for you, is what keep her in harm's way always. So, whatever you do slow it down and if you can just stop! If not change your patterns with everything from your phone, to your cars, shit if you can even change the way you walk, and dress do it!

Stone heard all he had to hear from this man to tell you the truth he had enough of this man. He thanked him, got up, and paid him for his service.

As he walked off from the table Antonio called him. "This is too much Stone; I don't need all this money."

"To much money for who Antonio I only paid what I felt you deserve." He did not even turn around to face Antonio as he spoke to him.

Stone kept walking and Antonio called his name again waiting for Stone to turn around. "Cheryl's son Loose approves the two of you being together for he knows you will take care of her the way you do with everybody."

"What makes you say that out of all things I told you?"

"Because he asked you to take care of his mom Stone. Now go with your heart and always follow your golden rule!"

Stone laughed a little then asked him what he was talking about.

"You know Stone trust no one and I mean it, at least no one in the game you are in." Those words let Stone know this man probably did had a gift for reading dreams or people. Then he brushed that thought off quickly telling himself this man was a thief and a liar. The crazy part of it all though was that he believed every word he told him and was not believing what he was saying to himself.

CHAPTER 15

The only thing Cindy has in mind today is to go shopping. She is going to get something sexy to wear tonight. So, she can surprise Stone when he calls her to meet up. She has so much love for Stone. To the point that her emotions have been affected as of late. She knows Stone very well and if he has not been around. Another female is pleasing him sexually. But at the end of the day she knew better than to mix business with pleasure. Besides, that will be Stone's excuse anyway. That was always his excuse to not hurt anyone feelings.

China has been staying with Cindy for a few days now. There is no way that she was not going to see Stone when he comes around. She made it her duty to hang with Cindy until she sees him. China was driving her new pearly white Lexus IS 250 in mid-town Manhattan. This is where she went to do all her shopping. To get all the top designer clothes. Cindy knew for a fact China was around for her personal reason. Only because she asked her numerous times about Stone whereabouts. As they got out of the car in the parking lot. Cindy began a conversation with Stone as the main topic.

"China, let me ask you a question. Do you think Stone has been acting strange lately?"

"I feel like that about him at times. He has put a lot of distance between all of us lately. I guess he has his reasons for doing what he do. But it does not stop me from seeing how he is moving with everyone. Cindy do you think he plans on cutting us off?"

"I am going to be honest with you. I really do not have an idea what Stone is up too. I hope whatever he is doing, will be beneficial for all of us. It takes lots of responsibility to be a boss. He has to keep the ball running." Although Cindy can relate to the way China feel about Stone. She is going to hold that conversation with Stone face to face.

"I hope you are right about him Cindy. We can't get all stressed out about it. For the simple fact, there is nothing we can do it. So, let's just do what we can control." She giggled as she went into her pursue. Pulling out a bankroll the size of a baseball. "We can go out here and spend some off this easy money."

The girls went into a couple of stores. Only finding a few items worth purchasing between the two.

When Cindy received the call, they both been waiting on. There is not a soul that can get them too stop shopping. With the exception of one person and that is Stone. These women are the pinnacle of what a shopaholic is. As she answered her phone her heartbeat accelerated. The palms of here hands got sweaty. "Hey Stone, how are you doing?"

"I'm doing pretty good Sin. I need you to stop what you are doing. Come to the Marriot Hotel, the one that is located at New Rock City. Please Sin don't have me waiting all day. I'm under a Carlos Sanchez in room 504. I'll let the front desk know that I am expecting you."

"I'm on my way to you right now. Just know I am coming from mid-town. So, it will take me a little longer then you expect. Is it cool if I bring China with me?"

"It's that a trick question? Of course, you can bring China with you. I will let the front desk know I am expecting two beautiful ladies instead of one."

"Yeah whatever Stone, I see you in a bit" Although Stone could not see her. She rolled her eyes at him. As she hung up the phone, she blushed a bit. It was just the effect always had on her. "Come on China let's get out of here. We have to go to New Rochelle to meet up with Stone." That was all she had to tell China. She dropped the clothes on a rack and stormed out the place. As the girls walked out of the store in a hurry. They never expected to see who was walking in. X and Chico where walking in to do a little shopping for themselves. Since the girls are in a hurry to get to Stone. China walked into Chico making him drop his phone.

Chico being the ignorant individual that he is. Yelled out loud causing a scene at the entrance of the store. "Watch where the fuck you walking you dumb bitch." Chico did not know who the girls are. It didn't really matter because manners is not a quality he has.

"Who the fuck you think you talking to, you sorry ass nigga." China then walked up on him and got all up in his face. The moment Cindy saw that the other male was X. Her attitude changed realizing that those amongst her are foes.

"You better put a leash on him before I put him down." As she said that her left hand went into her bag. In which she gripped her baby .9mm. "You know how I do it X." Blowing a kiss to X maintaining her poker face.

X for a fact knew that these women will shoot. He did not want to create a domino effect. Due to Chico always making bad decisions. "Fall back my dude, let's just get what we came in here for. Don't mind him Cindy he meant no harm. Everything is just a big misunderstanding."

"Well make sure your peoples understand who I am. Today will be the only easy pass I give any of you. Come on China let's get the hell out of here." Cindy grabbed China by the waist putting a separation between the two. As she walked off from X and Chico. She turned around and stared at X before winking at him.

It pissed X off for the fall out he has with Cindy. He was not going to let no female be the reason for any setbacks. The last time she nearly sent him back to the essence. He will be damn if he would let it happen twice.

The girls walked into the parking lot jumping into China car. Within the hour they arrived in the parking lot of New York City's Marriott.

Stone was sipping on Hennessy as he smoked joints of mango Kush. The television was on the sports center channel. But he was not paying any attention to it. He was more attentive to the music he was listen too. There was two artist that stood out for Stone the most. One by the name of Sky Soprano from Brooklyn, New York. The other a Central Florida artist by the name of Caskey.

There was a loud knock on the door. In which he knew very well who is knocking. It's Cindy that is at the door banging. Like if she was a person two times her size. He loves this girl to death and will do anything for her. He also has love for China, but it is not the same. Together as a team they are his guardian angels. But it's Cindy that forever will be his ride or die girl. He swore to always protect them. Making sure they will win in life.

He ran to the door answering it in his boxer's. The day get sunny every time he lay eyes on the two. These females are both beautiful, intelligent, and ready for whatever. No one can ask for troopers like this, bad, and deadly. He already made up his mind. That when they leave from this hotel. They are going to have to take care of a target. But first he is going to make sure they get time with him. Killers or not these beauties are very sensitive.

China and Cindy almost have the same taste when it comes to fashion. With their own little twist of originality. Today they dressed down with jeans and Jordan's. But it did not stop them from looking good.

"Damn I almost forgot how fine the two of you really are." Thinking of the last time the three was together. Gave him an instant hard on.

"Nigga please, you could never look this good." China gave a few poses for Stone. When she realized Stone was already getting an erection.

"What, you need an invitation to come in?" Stone moved out of the doorway so they can walk in. As the girls passed by him, he slapped them both on the ass.

Then gently caressed their rears kissing them softly. Cindy went a little extra by stroking Stone with both hands. Stone pushed her off him only so he can lock the door.

Stone got straight to the point with the girls. By the time he got to the master bedroom. He grabbed China by the waist and pulled her into him. He kissed her deeply while he slowly took her clothes off. Out the two girls, China has the edge on Cindy in looks. But it's Stone opinion only on their appearance. The history that Stone and Cindy have cannot be replaced. So, their bond is what gives her the edge over China any day. China got so excited, she helped him take her clothes off. Today is different, she has never wanted Stone so much. The thought of having him leave without ever returning was something she dreaded. Every second she spends with him has to be treated like it could be their last moment. She plans on giving him all of her. It was only to leave an impact on Stone. One in which he would think about when she is not around.

She kissed him slowly caressing his body. The moment he got fully erected she dropped on her knees. Giving him pleasure with her mouth. Cindy kissed Stone on the back of his neck; reaching around him to grab the back of China head. Pulling her on to his growing as she nibbled on his shoulders. It was going a little too fast for Stone. This is not his main reason why he has the girls here. He gently got them off of him. Telling the girls to get in the Jacuzzi. While he got them a drink and rolled a blunt of that fire.

As he broke the weed down to roll up a blunt. The girls utilized the time by keeping themselves warn. They kissed and played with each other. Keeping themselves warm and wet for when Stone is ready.

Stone lit the blunt and did not pass it. Until he was able to feel the high of the weed. He then passed the blunt to Cindy. Sex was always better when they are under the influence. Once officially high they took the action to the bed, in which lasted a few hours.

Stone order food and that is when Cindy brought up the conversation of seeing X in midtown. "Stone you know who I saw today? That lame ass nigga X! I swear to you that man is still scared of me." Just thinking of the way, he gets around her. Makes her laugh like a little girl. "His peoples was with him and cursed China out. She bumped into him making him drop the phone. At first it appeared that he was going to get aggressive. That's when I checked the two of them. X knew I was strapped, and he already knows I won't hesitate."

Stone was just glad Cindy was able to keep her cool. "So, what happened?"

"Nothing, the bitch came out of him. He basically said sorry for his friend's actions."

"You know what I find so ironic? I want you to find out who is X's connect. For some reason I think Bump is the person supplying him. I'm telling you he's playing a dangerous game, if he is the one dealing with the enemy."

"Well, I am going to be honest with you. I never trusted Bumpy only because he is over ambitious. Don't you see he is the only one that has a problem with keeping order amongst us. It will not surprise me if he would be doing some under hand shit. You must never forget that this is the streets. So, when you dealing with more than a handful. Believe me there will to be a Judas in the circle."

That's the second time in as many days. That someone said something negative about Bump.

"Stone, China is right about Bumpy. The man always has a problem with your shot calling. You don't see that every time you make a call. For some reason he goes against the grain. It's not that you are making the bad call for all. It's that he has a problem with following the chain of command."

"I never expected to run this like a dictator. I just see it as Bumpy being him. But if that is the case, then we must catch him red handed. keep this between us and God. You also need to remember that we cannot take Bumpy lightly. I know for a fact if he is rocking with X. Then he is ready to deal with whatever are the repercussions." He looked at China and noticed she gained a few pounds. Although they were having a serious conversation, Stone changed the subject. "Damn China, the extra pounds you gained look good on you." He walked up to her just to palm her ass.

China got very nervous that Stone notice her weight gain. This is not the time for her to talk about it. She wants it to be in private. So, for the moment she will not say a word. She is going to play it, the way she needs to play it. "Maybe it's because you have not been around to work this ass out."

Now that Stone said it Cindy also noticed her weight gain. "Stone is not lying about you getting thick, bitch. But it looks so good on you."

"I guess living the life the way we live it. You can't expect anything less from us. We out here in these streets eating like a mother fucker."

Cindy began to laugh high fiving her. "You know that's right China."

Stone grabbed China and pulled her towards him. He had enough of the talking and wanted to get off again. He spun her around and pushed her to the bed. She knows Stone wants her in the doggy style position. He penetrated her from behind taking his time. China has the pussy you never want to get out of. He took his time with every stroke. Enjoying the firm grip she has him in.

As Stone sexed China, Cindy watched as if it was a porno flick. She sat there watching the man she loves, make love to her friend. The only bitch she will ever trust in these streets. Now that Stone brought it up, the extra weight is obvious. Could it be that she is conceiving Stones child? It would pierce her soul if that is the fact. Not because Stone got china pregnant and not her. But because China can have a child and she can't.

After a few minutes Stone made groaning sounds that Cindy knew too well. He was cumming inside of China, she must be pregnant!

CHAPTER 16

The DJ had the club jumping all night. The music he played kept the ladies on the dance floor. It also kept the niggas spending on liquor. To make sure they leave out of there with a jump off. Blast was shining in the club with Murder, and Pretty. They maintained the bartender busy bringing bottles. It's rare that you see them go out, only cause they be on the grind hardbody. But when they do go out, they always do it right. After they lost Loose, they realize they can't be strictly business. One never knows when they will be taking their last breathe. So, they decided that every now and then. They will take time out to enjoy themselves with all the cheese they getting.

They were no longer the same people that started in the game. Today, they stand as made men in the business. No longer having the financial worries they once had. They went out tonight only to make a statement as a team. Standing strong in the cut, fly, with no worries.

Blast is feeling the moment, drunk as hell. He has been talking nonstop for ten minutes. Appreciating life with all that they have endured together. "We all need to be thankful that we're still alive. Look at us, we came up a long way. There isn't many people that set goals like us and succeeded. Don't you think so apeys?

"You already know the answer to that Blast. Forget about everything and let us enjoy the moment." Murder popped another bottle pouring it to the entourage of females. "The night always ends better when the ladies get white girl wasted." Murder popped another bottle calling Pretty. "Come here my brother, I want to share this bottle with you.

Pretty bagged a jump off already. A pretty Asian female that was ready for whatever. He was talking her into bringing her friends with her. When Murder called him too take a drink with him. He must do it otherwise will never shut up.

"Hear me out my brothers." Murder spoke in a slurred voice due to the alcohol he has consumed. Pouring a glass for Pretty as well as Blast. Then he held the glass as he spoke. "This is to us my beloved brothers. That always we will remain loyal to one another. But most importantly that we all stay true to the game. We all know that the only way we can weather the storm. Is if we play the game according to the rules."

"What you are saying right now is a fact, Murder. All I want, is for us to make it out. That we find a way out of these streets, successfully. The chances of us all getting out unharmed is one in a thousand. So, we going to go extra hard and trust no one. We are going to give it our all. In order to make sure we the first to do it."

Pretty just looked at them like they stupid. He knows what they are talking about is only wishful thinking. How we do the shit we do. Then think we will grow old to talk about it. Pretty knew there will always be negative consequences to their actions. But he did not want to spoil the moment for them. Because he understands the alcohol is getting the best of them.

That's when Blast drunk ass began to get emotional over Loose death. "Damn I miss my boy Loose. If one of us could of only ride with him."

"Then the chance that one of us would not be here. Could be a very high possibility. Talking about Loose have any of you seen Cheryl?" Pretty waited on Blast to answer him the question.

"To tell you the truth, I have not saw her since we got back from Puerto Rico. It's not like I saw her on the regular basis anyway."

"Well, wherever she's at I hope the best for her." Murder did not want to talk about Cheryl or her whereabouts.

Pretty had enough of the small talk with the fellas. He went back to the Asian female. Besides, they all had an idea with who she was with. But since it was Stone, they preferred to act dumb. This is one of those topics that it's best to not talk about.

X, Bump, Red, and Chico where on their way to the same club. The same club that Blast and company where in. Red rode shotgun with Bump, in his new Benz wagon. While Chico was riding with X in the new 500 Benz. As of late Bump and Red have been hanging tough. The two have a lot in common, besides being in the game. They are two of the same kind of people. The kind that will never let you know what they are thinking. They move in silence with high volumes of action. But at the end of the day, money is the motive. That is the only motivation to get into the game. If it's not about the paper, then there was nothing to talk about.

"I'm not trying to be in here all-night Bump. You know how I feel about the club scene. It's a place that brings too much attention. This is where all the pigs be going to watch mother fuckers. What better place to see who is getting money for real? You see hustlers in the club spending and tipping big. Niggas can never spend money that they don't have. But if you have it to spend it. Then the club is where you see people spend it."

"Don't get me wrong, I totally feel what you saying. But we also need an escape at times, real talk. With all the shit we be going through in these streets. We will always need a break, here and there. I tell you what, as soon as we get some pussy for the night. We be out of the club, cool?"

"That's a bet, let's go up in there and do this fast. We can go in there and get us some bitches for the night in no time. You know us my G, we look like money."

They got to the club and X partying ass went straight to the dance floor. He was always one of those dancing mother fuckers that could light up the dance floor.

Pretty was drunk, but the moment X walked into the dance floor he spotted him. He walked out the dance floor without hesitation. For the simple fact that he knows not to be around X for a second. His loyalty will always go to Stone without ever compromising it. He walked off the floor and told Blast who he just saw.

"Yo Blast, that nigga X is on the dance floor. I just saw his lame ass dancing."

The fact that X is in the club sobered Blast instantly. "Where the fuck did you see him at?"

"He's on the dance floor, you can't miss him."

"I'm ready to man down that nigga where he stands. Blast I'm getting the hammer, fuck that shit." Murder was always quick to resolve everything with violence.

"Fuck you talking about Murder? You know your ass will be in jail the moment you pull that trigger. Look around you, all eyes is on us."

"You sound like Stone all of a sudden. What's up with that? You talking to me like if I don't know what the fuck I'm doing."

"I am not saying you do not know what you doing. Nor, I am trying to be Stone. All I am saying is stay here with Pretty. While I go see what that nigga up too."

Blast observed X from a distance to not be seen. He played the cut out of X's radar, observing his surroundings. He maintains a close eye on X waiting until he finish dancing. This is the only way he can see who is with him. How can you get at him? When you do not know what you are stepping into.

Blast almost lost his cool when he saw who was with X. Bump was a part of their four-man team. Blast thought fast and took a few pictures with his phone. Just in case if Bumpy tries to deny the fact. He had the evidence he needed to show Stone. Who Bumpy is dealing with and what he has been up to. He saw enough and went back to the fellas.

"You not going to believe who is chilling with X."

"Who chilling with him?" Murder asked hyped ready to put some work in.

"This nigga Bump! I even asked him if he wanted to go out with us tonight. He told me he was going to take it easy for the night. To tell you the truth, it looks like he fucks with him."

"Let's go over there and go ape shit on them right now!"

"Let me call Stone and see what he wants us to do." Pretty then dialed Stone number to give him the news ASAP.

Stone picked up the phone on the third ring exhausted. "What's up lil bro how you?"

"Pissed off big bro at what I just found out and am witnessing. I'm calling to tell you that Bump is in the club hanging out with X. What do you want me to do to them bro?"

"Just chill and tell me where you at. That's all you got to do for me Pretty." Although he kept calm his mind went into war mode.

"I'm in the downtown spot we always talk about."

"Say no more just stay out of his view. I'll be there as soon as I can." Stone hung up the phone and told the girls to get dressed quickly. "We got to take care of something real quick."

The girls did not say a word to Stone. It has been

a long time that anyone seen him this upset. So, they already knew shit was going to get real. They did not say a word cause they know how Stone gets when he is upset. On the way to the club Stone went to get the Dodge Charger. That's when the girls knew shit might get real ugly. Because he always kept that car loaded with five P.90 Rugers.

Sin was actually glad that they might have to get their hands dirty. This is a team in which she knew her position. These are the streets and at times when you get paid without doing anything. It becomes a conflict of interest later in the game. As long as she gets her hands dirty, she knew she would be earning the money she be making.

On the way downtown Blast called Stone to let him know that Bump and one of the dudes left the club with three females.

"Well fuck him because we know where he lives at. Just keep your eye on X and don't lose sight of him."

"I got you on that beloved! How about if they leave the club?

"Then you follow them but please Blast. Don't let him out of your site."

"Say no more my brother, you know how I do. I stay on my job, always."

Twenty minutes later Stone called Blast to let him know that he was outside the club. They came outside and saw that Stone had the Charger. "Oh, it's about to get real ugly. That is what the fuck I am talking about." Murder said, ready for whatever come their way.

"Get your cars and wait for my orders. We are not going to do anything right now. All I want to do is know where the fuck he lives at. So, then I can deal with them accordingly."

They went into a parking lot because the streets of Manhattan stay busy. China stood across the street of the club being the spotter. She ordered coffee and sat in front of the restaurant. Sitting on a table where she could see who comes out of the club. An hour later the two walked out the club to the parking lot where Stone is in. They walked towards X car and jump in without looking at his surroundings. They just got in their car and drove off.

They trailed them from a distance communicating thru phones. Each of them taking turns tail gating to not get noticed by X. This is a chance of a lifetime for Stone. In which he does not want to mess up. As Stone trailed him in the car he thought of Bump.

X stopped in Harlem on 140th in Lennox to drop Chico off. That's when China told Stone that was the man that she bumped into that cursed her out. But then Cindy checked real quick on the spot.

"That's him China", Stone asked pointing

at the man. "What do you want to do with him babes? you know that's going to be your problem to handle?"

"I want to send him back into the essence Stone. The way he spoke to me clearly lets me know he has no respect for women. So, for that alone I want the privilege of doing it myself when its time."

To be honest you can do it whenever you want cause eventually, he will be a problem to us anyway. So, whenever you feel the time is right strike! But I want Bump and X for last! The first thing we do is take care of his soldiers and hurt their pockets. So, they could suffer a little before meeting their maker, then I will take those two out myself.

"Fuck all that bullshit Stone I say we take their asses out now! Why wait for another time when they right here right now! Truth be told if X had the shot at you, he will not hesitate to take your head off on the spot and you know that babes" Sin stated.

"Calm down baby you know that mistakes are not allowed this deep in the game they come out to costly. We worked way too hard to lose everything over a mistake. Besides they not in my level to find a way to get at me anyway. At the end of the day I'm playing chess with them not checkers, I keep telling ya that!"

"Well my dad always told me that he rather get

judge by twelve then carried by six. Right now, he may have life in prison but he is still breathing."

"I understand but just trust me on this one they will get what they have coming no matter what!"

Since he stopped in front of a building Stone had to keep moving up the block. But

thank God Blast was on point he maintained a good distance the moment he saw him make a right on 140th. When X pulled off, he was able to follow him from a distance and give Stone there location.

X pulled up into a beautiful house in Riverdale, got out the car, and walked into his freshly purchased house. For Stone this night was a success he got the answer to all the questions he wanted to know. Now what he was going to do was on him to strategies and the rest to follow through. But one thing was for sure X time on this Earth will soon come to an end.

They drove to China's apartment in Park Chester smoked a few blunts and that's when Stone got straight to the point. "Cindy, China, I want the two of you to take care of the guy that ya had a fall out with the other day. Pretty I want you to play Bump like white on rice. I don't give a fuck if he has to take a shit wait for him by the door. Murder I want you to find out about all the spots that are not ours that have good quality dope. See who is doing the drop offs and try your best to find out where the stash houses are."

"What do you want me to do?" Blast asked.

"Well just do what you have been doing, get money, be careful, take care of yourselves and keep me posted on what be going on in the hood. One more thing use your judgment wisely on everything that goes on from here on out. The process of elimination with our foes will begin real soon!"

"Stone are you sure that you don't want me to take care of Bump?"

"I'm positive about that one Blast, Bump is mine!

It bothered him that Stone was not as aggressive as he once was. It's like he does not know what Bump is really capable of doing. Blast was just hoping that with all the money Stone was seeing didn't make him soft.

A little while back Stone would have gone crazy with what is going on now. If this was the new Stone; Blast did not like him. But since it's Stone he was going to get the benefit of the doubt for sure.

Stone knew that they all expected him to handle things in a more violent manner. But for some reason he was taking heat to what Antonio told him. As far as moving and doing things different from his regular routine. But there is one thing for sure Bump would pay the piper for dealing with X, that no good backstabbing mother fucker.

CHAPTER 17

Stone called Santos to let him know he wanted to see Manolo in person.

"Why what's up Stone is everything alright?, I don't understand the reason for such a request."

"Don't worry I'll explain to you everything the moment I get to Miami." This was Stones first time going to Miami since killing the dirty cop. It shocked Santos that Stone wanted to see Manolo since everything was going so well. He didn't stress it cause he knew in a short time Stone will be telling them his reason for being in their presence.

Before contacting Santos he made sure Eduardo was already paid for the last load they gave him on consignment. Eduardo did not understand why he told him not to bring him product, but Stone explained to Eduardo that he had a lot of work left that was his profit. Every time money came in, he put it on the side to have Manolo's paper first and got in the habit of doing it in that fashion and for a second lost track of how much drugs he had. At least that is what Stone told him his reason for not wanting more work.

"Eduardo you don't understand I got to finish everything so that I can put my money on the side to reap my benefits. I also don't want to make matters more complicated than they are already."

"That's cool Stone you should be able to get your money and put it on the side. I don't see no other reason why we are in the game that we are in if it's not about the money. God knows we would have been working a job that we would have not liked for the rest of our lives if it was like that!"

"You not lying about that Eduardo if it's not about the money then I don't see our reason for taking so many chances." They held that conversation the night before now today he was on his way to see the top dog.

As far as Santos he did not like the fact that Stone wanted to speak to Manolo when he oversaw their negotiations. Besides they have a little more history then the one Stone shares with Manolo but here it is Stone wants to go through him to speak to Manolo. Well Stone has earned the right to do so, he told himself. So, the next thing he had to do was call Manolo to let him know there golden child was on his way down to see him personally.

"Well call me when he's down here ready to speak Santos."

Manolo did not have a clue of why Stone was on his way down to see him. All he knew was that whatever Stone had to talk to him about was not to his benefit because if things where good then Stone would have not travelled a yard and spoke to him over the phone. I just pray everything is well I would hate to have to change players when all is well at the moment.

Stone was going to Miami without saying a word to anyone. When he told Eduardo he still had merchandise he didn't lie to him, but he did not have any coke left. All he had was three keys of heroin and he had a purpose for those three keys.

He gave Sin a duffel bag that had a little over two million dollars and told her to put it away. He didn't tell her what was in it but one thing for sure was he knew she would not look in the bag and it was in good hands with her. The money was safe with her and he knew it for sure. Truth of the matter is that if she knew it was money in the bag the shit would still be safe with her anyway.

By the end of the night Stone was in the presence of Manolo in his estate.

"So, what brings you down here to speak to me so urgent about? I truthfully thought our program was running well to the point we are all happy, we are all happy aren't we Stone?"

"Yeah for sure money is coming in and things are going well Manolo. But the problem is I need some time to take care of the structure I personally have. There are a few things or people may I say that need taking care of and since it's so close in my circle I need some time out so that I can take care of it correctly and discreet."

Manolo was not trying to hear none of the shit he was talking. He has invested in Stone too much to hear that come out of his mouth. "Stone you need to understand that I only have you to take care of my business. Since you oft that cop, business in Miami went bad for everyone. You just can't decide to stop only because you are dealing with small issues in your circle. Besides things are going so well for us right now why spoil it?"

"Because I need some time out Manolo, I don't want to rush what I am about to do.

Don't worry as soon as I'm done with what needs to be done, we will be back to full swing of things."

"Stone I want you to know as a man I respect how you are conducting your business. But as business that is really bad for me. I have my shipment in New York with the understanding that you are my reliable source to get rid of the tons that's already up north. What you think the cartel will say if I tell them what you just told me? Well they won't say a word to me I'll be somewhere rotting with a Columbian neck time as well as my family. You think I will let that happen? NO!," Manolo yelled from the top of his lungs. "Now Stone let us not regret the day we met," Manolo just let him know what will happen if he did decide to chill for a while.

Stone was highly upset that Manolo spoke to him in that fashion. It didn't matter to him that he was the one that helped Stone reach his financial success being his supplier. "You know what Manolo it's cool I'm going to finish what's in New York but after that I'm done, you got that?" He tried to sound convincing but in his heart, he knew the only way to stop this relationship is through death.

"You're done when I tell you are done Stone, you got that Stone? I'm no street punk Stone don't forget that. I'm way over your league boy I made you so the truth of the matter is that it will be as easy as stepping on a roach to get rid of you."

Stone was no fool he expected this to happen, so he was ready for plan B. "Well then give me the help I need to take care of my problem."

"Stone you should have said that in the first place and we would of have to take it where I took it.

Santos!" Manolo yelled for him and he got there in two seconds sharp like always.

"Yes" Santos replied, "is there anything that I can help you with?"

"Get ready for the big city there is money to be made for you. We also don't know how long it will be for so go comfortably."

Stone didn't say a word he knew that without him Manolo probably would have not been standing as tall as he is right now. So, if somebody has to go first it would have to be Santos.

As Santos went to do what he had to do to get ready to go up north Manolo apologized for getting a little rowdy with Stone.

"It's not a problem I'm not the type to take things personally Manolo. I know you have a business to run and from one businessman to the other it's all water under the bridge."

"I'm so glad that you are a rational man Stone. I also know you are a man of honor by the way you conduct your empire. Another man would have let his pride be the end of him."

Stone was not dumb he now knows for a fact that the only way out with dealing with him was through death or prison. Unless he gets rid of Manolo and do what no one else was able to do and that's killing him through war!

About ten minutes later Stone and Santos where on their way to New York. As Santos was leaving the estate, he got a funny feeling like he was not going to see this place again. For the first time in a long time he felt nervous and he didn't know why. He looked over to say something as they passed the estate gates and saw pure evil in the eyes of Stone. Something inside him was telling him to stay in Miami but he went against his feelings. I'm the saint of death he told himself to confirm he will be good no matter what comes his way. I will not fear evil for I am evil itself.

Back in New York, Stone set up Santos in the best hotel suite and told him to stay under the radar until the time come for his services.

"The time for what Stone? now tell me why did I exactly come to New York for?"

"To take care of hood justice that is needed to be taken care of my friend. Don't worry the time will come sooner than later so you will not have to be here long."

"Oh, I'm not worried for I know I will get compensated well. We are veterans so we know for sure time is money."

"You know it! Stone jumped in a cab and knew three men had to die outside of his circle they are Santos, Manolo, and Eduardo as well. It must happen to them cause that would be the only way for him to be able to leave the game. As far as everyone else they small fries but these three are the type to get rid of his family the way Stone did to the cop down south. Till this day that was the only action that crippled his conscious of what he has done in the pass. He was a firm believer that you reap what you sew so he had to be real careful from now on out. He has done so much dirt to others that it was only right that the same will happen to him.

The first thing he had to do was go to his house and explain to his future baby mother Cheryl what kind of predicament he was in. As he pulled up into the garage as always, his two most loyal bitches were by the door wagging their tail. If people could be loyal the way dogs are, shit this world would most definitely be a better place.

He called Cheryl name when he walked into the house for it was dead quiet. She yelled out after the third time he called her name and let him know she was in the bedroom.

When he saw her in the bedroom, she was in her underwear looking at the mirror sizing her stomach up. "Do you think I'm getting fat?" she asked rubbing her belly.

"No ma you're pregnant there is a big difference between the two. But if you want to know you look so beautiful with a belly. As long as it's one that is bringing life cause if you ever get that big without bringing life it's over between the two of us."

"Shut up Stone why you being a jerk with me?"

"You know I'm just joking sweetheart don't get all sensitive with me. But there is some serious issues that I am going through right now that I would like for you to know about. So that you can give me the input I truly need and to be honest I really don't know who else to ask. But the truth of the matter is I find myself knee deep in the game without light at the end of the tunnel."

"So why you don't get out the game baby?"

"This is what I am trying to talk to you about babes."

He spoke without being interrupted by her. That's what he loved so much about her when he spoke, she always gave him her undivided attention.

He told her about knowing the only way he would be able to get out of the game would have to be tragic. He told her what kind of people he was dealing with and that he had to find a way out. Now he knew what Eduardo was talking about when he told him the crown is heavy. You got to make all the calls and deal with all the consequences.

"Well daddy you need to know there is always two ways to handle all matters. You can always do it the right way but most likely you will do it your way.

I just can't see you going to the police or running for the rest of your life. So, baby the only thing I could tell you is to get ready for war or be a slave to this man till you hit a brick wall through death or prison."

She was right there wasn't much of a choice for him either he stays with the program or go against the grain. As a man he knew he had to bring all he had to a man that Stone knew he would fall short to. Life or death he knew it was his self that put him in such a situation. So, it's only going to be him that will get him out.

"Look the only reason I am telling you this is so that you can know what I am into. A day might come when I don't return home and I will like for you to be prepared for the worst."

"Sweetheart is there anything that I can do? This was the same reason she did not want to take him serious at first. How dumb could she be that she believed death will not surround her being around Stone."

"Yes! I want you to take care of this house and stay here until whatever comes blow over. Keep this door locked at all time and never let anyone in. I don't care if it's the pastor from our local church baby. The people I deal with are very dangerous and I don't know what they already know about me. But if it's one thing for sure time will tell what they know."

"Of course, I can stay home and protect the house

that's going to be the home of our child. But please be careful sweetheart you know I can't go through loosing another love one this fast."

"Don't worry about that baby I'm not going to a grave no time soon. It's no way in hell I will permit that shit at all. I don't give a fuck who I am beefing with in the streets."

The dialogue they held got interrupted by a call from Bump.

"Yo what's popping Bump what have you been up to?"

"Chilling Stone I just want to know when we going to open up shop. The streets are going crazy you spoiled them and now they don't know what to do with the bullshit that is out there."

"Well we on hold right now it's not much we could do until we get more work. Just chill for a while and enjoy some of that money you been making."

"Well there is not much I can do but enjoy some of the money I made anyway. But you know what's better than that Stone? Making new money!"

"You not lying Bump but like I said we on hold. I'm pretty busy right now my dude I give you a call a little later."

"Yeah do that bro, talk to you," that's all Stone got to hear cause he hung up the phone.

"Cheryl, I got to get out of here and take care of

what we spoke about. I'm so sorry ma I didn't intend to have you imprisoned in your own home but please let's keep it like that till the storm clears out."

"It's O.K I'm a big girl, it would not be the first time I have to go under the radar to stay out of harm's way."

"Thank you for understanding babes I got to get up out of here and get this ball rolling on the A.M."

He turned the phone off and relaxed with Cheryl with his mind off the shit that was about to go down. He knows the odds are against him to the point where he might not ever make it back home. But that's the way it is and there is not much anyone can do about it. So, to stress it would be a waste of energy. In times like this you must chose to be predator or prey Stone chose to be predator!

The next morning Stone said his farewell to Cheryl and went to see his bro Blast. Cheryl cried a bit but understood certain matters have to be taken care of cause if you don't, they will take care of you.

Stone got to Blast's house, set up the chess board, rolled a blunt and started doing the politics with Blast. Everyone knows that with politics war comes and to be honest this is what Blast has been waiting for. They were getting all this money and Blast had really begun to think Stone got soft on them. But now he's glad to confirm that that's not the case.

"Now Blast I have given everything that is going on a lot of thought. We now know Bump and X are doing business when we all let it be known there is a zero policy to deal with that fool. But for now, we are just going to have the girls kill that Harlem cat."

"Why that dude Stone and not X, he small time."

"Because even though we know they are dealing together, we do not know who X is dealing with. How can we make a declaration of war without knowing who we are going to war with?"

Stone spoke to Blast about all that is going on excluding what had happen in Miami. He did not want to let Blast know his intentions was to get out the game. He has had enough of the streets and was wealthy enough to do something legit. A true hustler's motivation is to get into the game to get out of there financial struggle to do the things that one really wants to do. Sad but true unfortunately not everyone is lucky enough to go unharmed in the game.

"Santos killed that kid to bring Classic out in Brooklyn from the cut. Well we are going to do the same so that we can see who X is associated with."

"Yeah you right Stone it's not a bad idea because then at least we can recognize the faces of our bandits."

"Forget about being smart Blast it's about getting away with murder. We made all this money for us not to give it to a lawyer so he can fight for our freedom."

"You are one hundred percent correct on that one Stone, fuck it whatever it is we going to handle let's handle it correctly."

"Well bro I got to go shopping for a few outfits cause I'm crashing with you until our business is handle."

"Come on my brother you know my house is yours as well."

"I know that beloved, that's why I always loved you like a true brother."

"The same way here bro you know I feel the same."

CHAPTER 18

X has been spending a lot of time with Lisa and to his surprise she was a rider for real. He liked everything about her for one she was a very independent woman that took care of herself. After spending time with her what turned him on the most about her was that she always kept a Nina on her, a forty caliber at that. Then the sex with her my God was off the hook. It didn't take long for X to trust this girl and let her know his business freely.

"So, baby what's the agenda for the day are you going to be busy?"

"Not really, all I got to do is collect from wicked a little later so I might as well stay around until then. But after that I'm open for whatever."

Lisa saw right through Wicked the moment she laid eyes on him and knew he was the week link.

"That's good babes, since you have time open

could you please help me with a crate of nine millimeters I have. I want to sell those so I can get the motherload from my cousin in Tennessee."

"That's nothing girl you know guns sell themselves in the streets. That's something a broke person can change his money status real quick in the hood. So, people always like to invest in a gun so when money get tight if it ever do the solution will always be a quick come up."

"Cool! You know your cousin is getting out in five days?"

"Why you telling me something I already know Lisa. When he gets out, he is going to be taken good care of."

"Oh, I know X I didn't mean to get you all rowdy."

"You didn't, truth of the matter was that X got a little jealous of his cousin Chuck. Well anyway I got to go are you going to stay in the house or are you going out?

I got a thing or two to take care of, but I will see you later."

"Cool, just keep your phone on so when I try to call you it won't be hard to get in touch with you like always."

Little did he know her phone was turned off every time she was with her superiors.

X dumb ass was really falling for Lisa hard and

fast without really knowing her. Yeah, she's a freak in bed and did everything he wanted her to do without ever resisting. But the truth of the matter is she's no good for anyone in the game. He only kept her close cause he envied the way Stone moved with females that are straight killers and wanted to do what he did. On the low he admired Stone but at the same time hated him because he wanted to be him so bad.

Those are the actions that make X a lame instead of making choices on smart decisions he did them for a reputation. Truth be told those are characteristics that will send any man to the grave or prison rapidly.

X loved his new house it has everything he needs, and it was the only place where he feels safe, this is his kingdom. As he smoked a blunt of Cush, he told himself that for his next purchase he was going to put all his money up. Then that quick his thoughts went to Lisa and her fine ass.

Murder was on his job he always does exactly what Stone ask of him no matter what it is. From sun up to sun down he played the streets studying the flow of every drug spot that had a reputation of having a smoker stamp of heroin. In which did not have anything to do their enterprise.

Murder hired a few dope fiends to go from spot to spot testing bag after bag. For them it was a dream job to be honest it was more like heaven on earth.

These dudes where all put together by Blast pops and he let it be known that whoever could find out who is the supplier is going to earn twenty-five hundred dollars. Shit for that much money I could find out where the poppy seeds came from one of the dope fiends said. Another told Murder the dog food is the exact same shit that pops haves.

"Are you sure daddy cool that it's the same junk?"

"Look youngster I have been putting this shit in my veins longer then you have been alive. So, if I tell you it's all the same, it's the same. There possibly can't be two of the same fire dopes coming from different people now and days. I mean in the sixties maybe but now there is barely good dope in the game let alone two different distributers."

"Good looking then, find out who the supplier is who the supplier is and I wil compensate you heavy. Keep it all on the low and I will stay in touch through pops."

Stone went to see his mother, it has been a little while since he last visited her. He knows that his lifestyle puts her through a lot of stress and he did not like to lie to her when she asks him all the question she ask when he visits her. But the fact is he only lies to prevent her from stressing. He also ran from all the lectures she gave him of how he pollutes his people and rob them from their sanity. He also gets tired of hearing his dear mother telling him that he should get a regular job and live a normal life.

"Hey mami how are you?" he asked giving her a kiss and a big hug. For Stone she is and always will be the world to him for all that she has done for him while he was coming up.

"I'm fine the question is how things are going for you my beloved son?"

"Well, I guess, I just came over here to tell you that I love you very much and to ask you if you can put some money away for me in case a rainy day ever comes."

"No problem son you know you don't have to ask me for that baby."

He went to his car and came back with a large brown paper bag that had two hundred and fifty thousand cash.

The amount of money made her hysterical, "who did you kill to get this money?" she asked him on the verge of crying.

"Come on ma you know I hurt no one to get this money. You already know what I do in the streets to make my living."

"Baby if you got this money in the streets then that is a lot worse than hurting a person cause here you are destroying communities and families instead of one person."

'You probably right but if I won't get this money then somebody else would because one thing is certain there will always be drugs polluting our streets."

"So, what you telling me is that if ten people jump off the roof you going to do the same?"

"Mom please with all due respect I only came to drop off this money not to get yelled at by you." A slight smile appeared on Stone face that got his mother highly upset for she knew she did a better job on her son.

"You know what you're right son I will hold this money for you but make sure the next time you come it's to pick up your money. Please be careful cause lately I have been worried sick that something is going to happen to you. You know a mother knows, keep your eyes open and always remember a friend is a dollar in your pocket when you got it, they are around but when you broke there is not a friend in sight. So only trust God and keep an eye on everybody else."

"Thank you, mom I know, what you tell me is for my best interest. I am also sorry for putting you through all the stress I have been putting you through."

"Well if you really sorry leave the game alone and get an ordinary life with a good woman and get yourself some kids."

"Believe me mom that is exactly what I am going to do! But you know what you tell me all the time, don't say it just do it and that is exactly what I am going to do."

Stone really hated the fact that through the years all he did was hurt his mom. But he already made up his mind to raise his child with Cheryl and be out the game for sure. He wanted to tell his mother that he was going to be a dad but didn't only because the time was not right for him to speak on it. He thought about Cheryl and his team and was going to make sure they all will be set out properly before this was all over. At that moment he knew that whatever obstacle presents itself it would not stop him from getting out the game.

Bump has been getting tired of Pretty for some reason the man did not want to leave his side. At first it was cool to be chilling with him but surrounding himself around him has prevented Bump from taking care of the ventures he had going with X. He tried everything to brush him off to the point where he made it obvious that he needed his space but Pretty ignored the signs.

"YO Pretty what is up with you are you alright?"

"Why wouldn't I be alright Bump, Pretty did everything in his power to hide the way he really felt about Bump for he did not want to share the same air with Bump, but Stones orders was Stones orders."

"I don't know you haven't been the Pretty I know for some reason you look like you are mad at the world. It shouldn't be like that when we are getting money at such a high scale. If anything, we should be happy considering where we came from.

You think that I have not been the same old me," Pretty said smiling trying to throw Bump off. The truth is that Pretty just wants to blow Bump head off on the spot. The only thing that stopped him from doing it was because he was following Stones wishes. He questioned his wishes for a second and even though he did not agree with the way Stone is taking care of the situation it's Stone call that is going to get manifested.

"So, what is it that's bothering you Pretty, is it me?"

"Fuck you talking about stupid, it's just that I miss Loose that's all. Come on you know that he was my right-hand man when he was alive."

"I don't want to sound cold hearted, but you got to move on with your life and forget about Loose he needs to be let to rest in peace."

"That's easy for you to say." Pretty said in an angered voice.

"Fuck you mean it's easy for me to say. If you have to say something say it without biting your tongue.

You acting like Loose was not my peoples either," Bump answered getting all in Pretty face.

"I don't want to talk about that" Pretty said pushing Bump out of arms reach.

"You know what Pretty I talk to you later before one of us pass the line."

"Cool then I see you later," Pretty fought so hard to not lose his composure and do something to Bump on the spot for he knew if he did Stone would then be highly upset with him for not sticking to the game plan. Not wanting to upset Stone was what stopped Pretty from killing Bump on the spot. But little did Pretty know is that Bump was strapped at all times. He knew for a fact that he was playing a very dangerous game. A game that could explode on his face for playing both sides of the fence.

CHAPTER 19

The girls have been staking out Chico for the last couple of days. But the way he moves make it hard for them to pick the right timing to push his wig back. They have been doing their homework and waited patiently in front of his house for the past day and a half and still no signs of him.

"Cindy this mother fucker has not been in the house all day, where could he be at?"

"Wherever the fuck he is at, does not matter. When I see him his ass is going to meet his maker."

"You must be easy, we been out here too long you know countless people saw us out here and I am not trying to spend the rest of my life in prison for some-one that is not worth two cents."

"So, what you think is the best way to do it?"

"I say we wait for him in his apartment since we know he is not there right now. As a matter of fact, I have a cousin that is a lock smith he can open the door for us in no time."

"You fucking crazy bitch, but you know I like the idea. When can you have him get us in the apartment China?"

"I could call him right now and see when he can get here." They already found out which was Chico apartment by talking to a woman that stood in front of the building. She claims that she has be living here all her life. By the face expressions she made you can clearly see that she did not like Chico.

She called her cousin Michael and he agreed to be there within the hour.

It took him no more than 2 minutes to have the door open and be out of their way. She then gave him a grand and told him this never happened. He was just glad to have got some easy money. At the end of the day he knew he got paid only to keep what ever happened between them and God which he had no problem with.

As soon as they got into the crib, they quietly ransacked the place looking for items of value and money. Sin took care of the two bedrooms while China looked throughout the rest of the house. They searched everything from under the bed, sneaker boxes, the medicine cabinet, to food items. Sin was a little impressed for the place was kept up to par. It was as if he lived there with a family or something.

But it was just a routine he got used to from being in prison. A lot of times convicts like to stockpile their commissary and have tons of can goods just so that they can feel good about themselves in prison. It's like indirectly letting everyone else know that they have love ones in the street taking care of them. Don't get it fucked up savages live of the land as well.

They did not find anything of value, so they made sure what they touched went back into place. So that when Chico comes into his apartment, he will not find his place out of order.

"I'm not going to lie to you Sin, this dude is a fly mother fucker."

"What you expect? He is one of these fly ass Harlem cats. But what amazes me is that he keeps the house so clean with everything coming from top manufacturers, not bad for an asshole like him."

"Well where he's going, he is not going to be able to take any of this with him."

"You not lying about that Sin Any way let's get comfortable until he gets here."

Sin then went to the PS4 player turned it on and the television as well. She is going to smoke up some of his weed and watch a movie. As the CD played, she did not pay attention cause she called Stone to let him know that they are in position to get X's friend.

"That's what I'm talking about sweetheart just

keep me posted." That's all he said to her before the line went dead.

Then her thoughts went to Stone and how much she loves him. She still remembers the impact he has had on her life and the conditions he got her out of. Before him she lived from couch to couch not knowing where her next meal would come from. All of a sudden, this knight in shining armor came and scooped her up gave her a place to stay, a form to get financial freedom, so her loyalty goes out to him without ever questioning his shot calling.

She then sat down on the plush sofas and watched the movie. It got her off guard to know this man was so crazy to keep evidence like this that can incriminate him. It saddened her to have a person get so humiliated the way Chico did to the man in the video. The way the girl yelled you can tell that he took her virginity and created very deep scars for this young lady.

"Can you believe this sick bastard did this to a family? I'm really going to enjoy killing this man Sin I swear to you!"

"You could see in the man eyes that he was enjoying every bit of it. It's crazy how in our communities the most average person on the outside could be so sinister in the inside."

"China, we going to do this man dirty for all the

women that ever got raped on this planet I swear to you so if you don't want a part of it, I understand."

"Shut up bitch I am in this with you no matter what!"

Another day was passing by and still no signs of Chico. The girls got very tired and hungry but the hatred they feel for this man now would keep them up for another week. They wanted him so bad that they had a hard on for him.

"How long you think we have to wait for this man?" China asked.

"I do not know but I am staying here for as long as it takes China."

Chico had been partying all week and his body was in need of some rest. All he wanted to do was go straight to bed to get some rest. A shower can wait till tomorrow I don't give a fuck he told himself. As he walked into his apartment the feeling of him not being alone hit him. As he locked the door, he seen a shadow through his peripheral.

"Don't move you bastard or else I swear to God you won't have time to regret it."

Chico did what they said off top for he knew if this was a contract, they would have killed him already.

"You got it; just don't shoot me I am not going to try to resist. Tell me what you want me to do and consider it done. If you came here for money, then the money is in the speaker in my bedroom by the window."

"Well take me to it and if you try it then that's your ass."

"Oh, don't worry I'm no hero," he then saw that there was another person with this female and noticed he was getting had by a pair of bitches. He did so many of them dirty that he did not have a clue who they are.

They took him to the bedroom and told him to lay flat on his stomach on the bed. As soon as he complied one of the females got on top of him and cuffed him to the bed post spread out. The girls then checked the speaker and saw that they hit the jackpot.

"Now that you have what you came for get the fuck out my house and leave me the fuck alone."

"Not yet pappi the money was only a plus, the real reason why we are here has not been spoke upon yet."

Chico's heart was filled with fear for he expects the worse now. Being the crazy mother fucker that he is he tried to control the situation. But looking into their eyes he now understands he has met his match. Sin saw the fear clearly through his face expression which made her feel a form of power that she never felt before to be honest it was more of a high that she felt.

"You better think about what you doing cause I swear to everything", he never finished his sentence cause China gun butted him with her .40 Caliber.

"Please shut your mouth so we can play twenty-one questions. Mind you the answers you give me will determine the outcome of how you leave this earth. Either you go quick or slowly that I will leave it up to you! Unless you tell me what I want to hear, and I will let you live."

"So, ask me what you want I will tell you anything but please don't kill me. The bitch was coming out of him quickly the moment she gave him hope that he will live past the day."

"The first question that I'm going to ask you is very simple, who's X," Sin asked.

"I do not know a X," Chico answered, he knew they came for info and tried to be loyal to him, wrong move.

"Oh, you want to save him huh," Sin spoke to China without saying her name and told her to get a knife. China got it in seconds and that's when he became nervous and tried to let her know he will give him the right answer.

"Well let's put it like this the next answer you give me you will know better than to give me the wrong answer."

She used the knife to rip a hole through his jeans and boxers and what happened next will traumatize the most honorable men in this world. She inserted the tip of the knife into his rectum and promised him that the next time he says a lie she will rape him with it the way he raped the young girl in front of her family.

"You do know what I am talking about, too don't you?"

"Yes!" Chico yelled only cause he did not want to go out like that, and the girls embedded fear in his heart.

China gun butted him again and told him if he yells again, they will find him with a bullet in his head and a knife in his ass.

Chico politely begged for his life, but it went to deaf ears. These girls came here for a purpose that was going to be served no matter what.

Seeing him beg with teary eyes gave her a feeling like no other. She was doing this for all the women that got raped, mistreated, abused, and were never appreciated by men that took advantage of them.

"I am going to ask you one more time who the fuck is X?"

"He's my boss and that's the God honest truth."

"Now we getting somewhere, now tell me what roll do you play in his structure?"

"The enforcer, I get paid to keep this organization in order."

"Now who is X's supplier?"

"His name is Bump he's the one that keeps the flow of the narcotics."

"Good boy," Sin said spanking him on his behind in a playful manner. "Now tell me who is the main runner and don't give me no runaround."

"Well the only other person that do the run around is this guy from Watson avenue that goes by the name of Wicked."

Before she could ask him Wicked address, he spilled the bean to save his ass. He let them know Wicked address, who lives there, and that he really was no threat the only reason he had such a position was because he's X lackey.

"Are you sure that you telling me the truth and you just not giving me the runaround?"

"Yes, I am positive you fucking," he stops in mid-sentence cause Sin jerked the knife.

"O.K, O.K you got it," I am sorry Chico pleaded for is life.

"Now this is going to be the million-dollar question so do not hold back or that's your ass. So, think good and get right what I am about to ask. Who does Bump get his product from?" She only asked cause she wanted to know how much they knew of Stone if they knew anything.

"His name is Stone, I do not know shit about him

but only that he is supplying damn near the entire Bronx. He is someone out of our circle he's more of an enemy to me than anything."

Sin did not like that Stones name was out there like that. Because it's a person's reputation that gives a rat the ammunition to tell on you. If no one knows what you doing, then no one can talk to the police and let them know your business. So, it's your reputation that plants the seed to your downfall in the hood.

"Is there anyone else I need to know about? Tell me home boy or forever hold your peace."

"There is one more guy by the name of Redrum, but he is a total shadow. There is no one that knows much about him all X has his number and he pops up as he is needed. So now since you know everything, I know, are you going to let me live?"

"I have to be honest my job was not to take your money or get info from you. My job was to do this," she pulled the knife out of his behind and stabbed him repeatedly in the neck.

Chico could not believe that after all the information he gave them they still are going to kill him. He was in complete horror trying to gasp for air, but it was no use. He tried to hold his neck but was unable to cause he was tied down.

Sin looked down at him and felt no pity for the

man she watched as he fought for air. All you heard was a gargling noise and after about two minutes his body went limb.

"China go to the DVD player and play the CD again!'

"Why you want me to play that bullshit again Sin?"

"I want to send police on a wild goose chase. That right there is called a motive so when the police see that they will think it came from them."

"Damn bitch that is so smart of you what made you think of that?"

"Forget about that babes and let's get the fuck up out of here. We can go to my place and divide this money up. Then we can put Stone on to what we know now."

They walked out of the building and to their surprise the streets of Harlem where empty. It was to their benefit that they went unnoticed. They laughed a little for it went all too well for them. They dumped their pistols in a garbage can right before they waves a cab down riding out into the night.

CHAPTER 20

Earlier in the day Stone was visited by Eduardo dropping him off a hundred kilos of cocaine and forty of heroin. He had to take the work, there really was not a choice for him. But if his game plan went well this would be one of the last times that he will get anything from him. One thing was for sure, he was planning an offensive strategy to take them all out. For the mean time he was going to play it safe.

He decided to go with Blast to see Santos and see how he is doing so far with his stay in New York. Like they say keep your friends close but your enemies closer, that is exactly what he must do, especially with Santos being the most dangerous man out of them all.

"So how has it been for you so far here in New York, Santos?"

"To be honest Stone the people here already got

me a little tired. For some reason they all deal with an attitude like if they are miserable to be alive."

Stone laughed at Santos for he remembers when he was glad to be here the first time around. But now it's a good thing he is seeing the true nature of a New Yorker. They are by far the most aggressive people in the world.

"Fuck everybody" Blast cut in; "it doesn't matter how the people of New York are. What matters is that the people you deal with are true to you. I know you really did not come to meet people; you came for business! So, wait till you get back to your place of action to get acquainted with others. You are here for a certain purpose that soon will be called upon. So, fuck the people and what they do cause none of them is putting money in your pocket."

"It's not about money all the time, don't you think? There will come a time that we are going to get judged by others or God. It will make me feel better knowing I treated people right until they ask for what they deserved. You should keep some sort of a conscious in this life. You don't want to end up in a gutter somewhere with a bullet to your head, having the world not giving a damn about you."

"Why do you care about all this shit all of a sudden? We are who we are and in this game, you already know we are fucked any way we live because of the things we do."

"Well with my God as I know him Blast, I know he will protect me through my darkest moments."

"I feel you Santos, your beliefs are your beliefs and you are going to do what you want. I just stay away from these never-ending conversations of spiritual views and what's right or wrong in this hell. But if you feel that way why do you do what you do Santos?"

"Because no one is perfect in this world and I love the lifestyle that I live."

"Enough of this lets go get something to smoke and eat so we could relax and have a few females come over." Stone did not want to get into all that bullshit, all he wanted was for Santos to relax so when the time come, boom, he'll be man downed.

On their way to do make their runs Stone received a phone call from China.

"What's going on babes, how you doing, is everything alright?"

"Everything is fine, but there are a few things that I need to speak to you about on a personal level. But it must be face to face, that is the only way that I am going to tell you what I have to speak to you about."

Stone had no clue what she had to talk to him about, but it had to be important for she knows there really aren't enough hours in the day for her to be wasting his time.

"Let me ask you have you seen Sin today?"

"Yes. She's actually been staying in my house; she is sleeping right now though. Look Stone I need to speak to you now, when and where we going to meet up should be our topic."

"Alright within the next hour I should be in the little spot that we get food at all the time, you know the one I am talking about, right?"

"Yes, I do, I am going to get ready and I will see you there." China got Sin up and told her to get dress that they are going to meet up with him at the end of the hour.

At first, she tried to protest telling her that she didn't want to go. China let her know that it was of great importance if she went with her but if she did not go, she was still going to meet up with Stone. In two seconds, sharp Sin was up not because she wanted to go but because China told her it was important to her and as a friend, she would ride out with her whenever she asks.

On the way to the restaurant Sin kept asking her what was so important for her to meet up with Stone.

"You will find out shortly Sin, but please stop asking so much I am not going to tell you till we there. So, you don't have to waste your breathe because you not going to make me change my mind."

"Fuck you then bitch," Sin got upset with the fact that she was holding out on her. After all the shit they have been through there is nothing that she is supposed to wait to tell her. The only thing that you can here for the rest of the ride was the radio playing.

His face lit up the moment he saw the girls stroll towards the table. Everywhere they went the attention they received from others was always the same, people looked at them with admiration. Then when they walked up on Stone and gave him the love that they do puts the icing of the cake. People could not believe that one man could handle so much women in the two of them.

Sin as always is the first to give him his hugs and kisses. But this time China made sure that it was her to get the attention first. Stone greeted them and told them to sit amongst them, then asked China what was it that she had to speak to him about.

"I have to speak to you not anybody else," she looked at Blast and Santos as if saying excuse, me in a polite fashion.

Blast picked up quickly and told Santos to go with him to smoke a cigarette. He knew that the girls had to speak in private and he perfectly understood.

"Well first and foremost we need to tell you about the Harlem cat."

"What about him" Stone asked "don't tell me there is a problem with him."

"There is a problem with him, but it is not our problem someone has to bury him" Sin joked.

"Well that is good news girls, I am glad to know that ya took care of it. Now tell me China what is it that you have to tell me?"

"Besides what we found out about X business I need to tell you," before she could tell him that she is pregnant Stone cut her off being excited that they got info from Chico before killing him.

"I'm telling you; I don't know where I would be if I did not have ya in my corner."

"Forget about that I am trying to tell you that I am pregnant but for some reason there is always something else more important to speak about." China could not hold back any longer and she pause for a second after realizing she put the news out there so bluntly. Sin looked at her in complete shock while Stone studied her to make sure she was not pulling his leg.

"I know you just did not say what I thought you said" Sin remarked angrily.

"I did, Cindy and I am very sorry I did not tell you earlier. But the reason for me saying it in front of you is to let the both of you know I am keeping the baby. I will not abort my unborn child and if you do not want a part of my child's life it is fine. I will leave today without ever having a problem or regret. I will raise my child somewhere else away from all the drama or harm's way."

"What makes you think that I will not play a part in my child's life. Did I ever give you the impression of a man that abandons his own? To tell the truth it makes me so happy that you are willing to give a lot up for my unborn child. That is the decision all mothers should make when it comes to their babies."

Sin was so upset with the fact that China was pregnant. But the truth of the matter was that she is the one that introduced the two so if anything, it was her to blame for what is going on now. It also saddened her that she was unable to reproduce life and give Stone what he has wanted for quite some time now.

China looked over at Sin then gave her a hug for she knew what Sin was thinking. She knew Sin wanted to be a mom so bad but could not possibly do it.

"We could both raise the baby as both of our child. You know how cool it would be for the baby to have two moms as beautiful as us?" She then looked over at Stone and asked him what they are going to do as parents.

"Well since you are going to have the child the first thing you got to do is get your ass out of the hood. Where you decide to go is what we have to agree on. I will not have my child grow up in the same streets where we are basically burning down for our financial freedom. After all the shit we did there are not too many people we can trust out here."

"Stone nobody has to know you are the father of this child."

"I know China and that is what's important to me. I will not have my flesh and blood nowhere but with me! I want to raise my child and play a part in his everyday life. Just pack your shit because in the next couple of days you are going to leave the shit you know!"

"What am I going to do Stone and where do I stand?"

"I do not know Sin it all comes down to what you want to do. Whatever makes you happy is going to be what I will support cause at the end of the day I care how you feel."

"I am going wherever ya go you already know that the only family I have is us!"

"I am cool with it, but you need to know there will be no coming back to the life that we are so accustomed to Sin. China is giving it up so she can be a mother. You have to make sure you want to do it for you."

"I am going to do it for us Stone" she hugged China then kissed him. Even though she was hurt that the man she loves is having a child with another woman she did not care because it was them that she wanted to live her life with.

As they came to an agreement of what they are going to do for the near future, Murder called Stone to let him know about the info he got on the streets from daddy cool and company.

"Well I am in City Island you know our little spot. Come and chill with us over here, there is no use to talk about what I already know. The girls got on their job and practically gave me the entire break down. It confirms what we already knew all along about Bump grimy ass."

"Word! They found out? You should have told me instead of me spending all that time and money. Fuck it Stone I be there in about twenty minutes."

The feds listened in on the conversation, they have tapped Murder's phone after he served an agent two times for weight. The only reason that he is not in jail is because they want to build a conspiracy case on the entire team and that right there takes a lot of time. So even though Murder could get arrested right now they did not bring him in. Them pigs stockpile cases on you so when the time come, they got you deep in shit where if your entire life will not be spent in prison a good amount of time will be spent behind those walls.

"Well Murder is going to meet up with someone that refuses to speak on the phone. So, he has to be someone of importance in Murder's structure."

"So, what you waiting for let's get moving and see who he is going to meet up with in City Island." Officer Rivera basically became a fed for its paycheck and the license to kill cause he could not stand another officer to even speak to him especially his superior. Every time a word came out of his mouth Rivera wanted to beat his head in. At the end of the day he is a criminal at heart and a pig during his work hours.

After eating the girls decided to start sorting out whatever they felt was of importance in their apartments. They knew Stone was a man of his word but most of all he was a man that took care of his business. So, they wanted to be ready for him and the only way of doing it is by packing now. like they say stay ready so you don't have to get ready. They knew when he says now it means now! So it was important for them to store what is of sentimental value for when he say it is time to go.

As they were going into China's car Murder was pulling into the parking lot in a Tahoe.

"What's good with you bitches Murder joked, He was always talking to them in that fashion, but he was just the pain in the ass little brother."

"Not much Murder just taking it easy, what's up

with you? Also do me the favor and watch how you talk to me and what you call me! I'm getting really tired of you the day is going to come when I am going to wash your mouth out with soap."

"You know the two of you are my sisters and I mean no disrespect. So, do me the favor and stop being so sensitive bitches."

"Yeah, I know Murder" Sin told him to let him know it was nothing. As the girls drove out of the parking lot they seen a suspicious car staying out of Murders view. When they drove by Sin saw that it was police in the vehicle. Oh, shit! She got on the phone and called Stone letting him know police are following Murder.

"Good looking Sin I tell you without ya I would have been dead or in jail already."

"No problem baby they are getting out of their car and it appears that they are going in." When she waited for an answer she noticed that the line was dead.

When Murder walked towards Stone, Stone told him to go to the bathroom and wait for instructions because he was followed here by pigs. Murder did not ask no questions he went to the bathroom and hid in a Stall.

Stone watched as two males walked into the restaurant that looked no different than any one of them. Damn these bastards look like any one of us Stone thought. He saw as they walked in quietly ordered drinks and looked around discreetly. If Sin would of not give him the heads up, he would have never thought them out to be cops.

Stone text Murder to instruct him to walk straight out the restaurant and don't say anything to him on the way out.

"Cool!" Murder walked out of there doing exactly what Stone told him to do. On the way out he looked around but there was no one there that he could mark as the police. As he walked towards the car Blast and Santos walked into the place coming back from the so call cigarette break. They got caught up kicking it to a few females they saw as they walked out to give Stone his time with the girls.

"I think they pointed us out," Rivera told his superior.

"Why do you say that?"

"Because he came in here went into the bathroom but never approached a soul. He then left the restaurant as soon as he got out of the bathroom. I know he did not come to City Island to use the bathroom. I think it was the females that drove out the place when we were coming in that pointed us out."

"So, what do we do now?"

"Let's stay put and enjoy our drink next time we have to be extra careful of how we tail anyone."

Stone looked at them and is so happy that he could point out the cops without them being able to do the same. It usually is the other way around and when one finds out that they are pigs onto them it be too late.

"Blast we have to take it easy from now on. You see those two dudes over there in the corner to our left. They the police and they followed Murder over here I guess to see who he deals with."

"How the fuck you know if we are all here together?"

"Because the girls put me on when they left the place!"

"So, what are we going to do now," Blast asked quietly?

"We are going to do the same shit we been doing. They are not on to us cause they have yet to make eye contact with me. They actually looked confuse when Murder walked out of here without speaking to a soul."

"So out of curiosity what are we going to do with Bump?"

"We are going to take care of him Blast but we must move slowly. Just give it a few you will see that time takes care of everything. You already know God didn't build the Earth overnight and that's God! So, let's play it safe and take our time with what we have to do. At the end of the day we must see what kind of police are on our trail. One thing is for sure whatever the plan is it's still going to get enforced but we just have to do it as if we walking on eggshells."

CHAPTER 21

X was on his way to pick his cousin Chuck up from Clinton Correctional Facility. He left at eleven thirty last night accompanied by Omar so it would give them more than enough time to get there. He knew that if they did not get there in time the Correctional Facility by law has to put you on the greyhound bus. Knowing Chuck, X would not hear the last of it if he has to travel in the bus after all the time he has just finish serving.

They went to the front office at 6:30 A.M to let them know that family members of Charles Vargas are already here to pick him up. So, there won't be no reason to put him on a bus.

An overweight guard let him know it's not release time yet with an attitude. That is the way these correction officers are up in the mountains with anyone other than their own. I guess that is a reason for them having a short life span once they retire. They eat and hate to much, two things that are definitely bad for a person health.

X ignored the man and left without saying a word to the fat fuck. He went to a near bye diner to get some food and chill until about eight o'clock. That is more or less the time that prisoners begin to breathe free air. Once in the diner Omar began to put his bid in with X. He knows X is getting a lot of money and he is starving to the point where he is ready to do whatever it takes.

"When are you going to put me on X? I am in real need of getting some money bro.

Times are so hard I am ready to do anything to get me on my feet."

"Trust me the time is coming real soon just be patient for a little more while. You know things like this cannot be rushed. It takes time to really get established out here."

"I guess I don't have no other choice X. You the only person that I know that is in a position to put me on. Just don't have me waiting for ever I'm starving in these streets" Omar joked. Even though he kidded to X he was serious about every word he said.

They took their time eating to kill the little time they had to wait for the facility to do it's paperwork that is needed so that Chuck can be released. Now that they knew he had family waiting for him the process was only going to take longer out of spite and X knew this.

As X and Omar waited for Chuck in the front of the prison Chuck walked out a free man looking like a million dollars in a designer suit. He looked more like a top-notch lawyer then a convict coming out of prison. They embraced each other, then X introduce Omar to his older cousin.

"Now let's get the fuck up out of here I am tired of seeing so many crackers. Take me back to the hood cuzzo that I have missed for so many years. I need to see dirty buildings and streets to feel at home that's word to my mother!"

As they drove towards the rotten apple X told Chuck to open the Glove compartment. He almost forgot about the gift he put there for his cousin. When Chuck saw what was there for him, he got short of words. Not only did he take care of him in prison but ten minutes from being released he gave him ten grand in cash and another twenty in jewelry.

"Thank you so much X you have been with me since the day you was able to hold me down and never left my side since. I really am so happy to have family like you." Even though X was driving the car it did not stop Chuck from giving him a hug that made him swerve two lanes on the highway.

"Chuck stop all that sensitive shit you almost made me crash! The only thing I am doing is what family is supposed to do for each other it's nothing special."

Halfway throughout the ride home Red called X to let him know about Chico.

"X they found Chico in his apartment with his throat cut with multiple stab wounds tied up to his bed. I always knew they was going to find him done dirty for all the extra foul shit he was doing."

"Get the fuck out of here Red when did this happened?"

"I am not sure, but it was a few days cause the neighbors where the ones to give a complaint from the stench that was coming out of the apartment. Now get this the authorities say that the motive is believed to be revenge."

"Revenge from who?" X asked Red not really caring what happened to him. His cousin has been released that is all the help he is going to need as of now.

"Remember the CD that he kept in the DVD player all the time? Well I guess what he did to those people bit him on the ass. The man did what he had to do for Chico rapping his wife and daughter. At least that is what the news stations are saying as of right now."

"Wow, that's crazy, Look I am on my way to the city I will call you when I get there. I'm just kicking it with my fams, so I'll holla at you."

"What happened X who did they killed in the hood?"

"They found one of my goons done dirty in his house. He is one of them dudes that did so much foul shit that nobody will ever know why they killed him. With him it was all a matter of time before it happened."

"What the fuck was he doing out there that you not even caring about that man life?"

"Let us not get into all that right now. You have not even made it home yet to get into all the bullshit. Put it like this, he reaped what he sowed do I need to say more?"

"You know what you are one hundred percent correct on that. Whatever he did is on him now it's my turn to do what the fuck I do best."

Stone was feeling a little paranoid by the fact that police was following Murder. He did not know how much they had on them as a team. One thing that is certain for sure, Murder was hot! He was not sure if it is because somebody in his circle went sour or if it came from an outsider. He had to reevaluate his game plan and strategize a new order to prevent a domino effect.

There are a few things that need handling in our structure. For one he had to get the girls out the radar and avoid something happening to them. He was going to have Murder get low for a little while as well. Iit meant that Blast and Pretty was going to take care of everything for the mean time. Until everything is orchestrated, he will let Bump be in his circle and supply X without any conflict. But he was not going to let everybody know that he was good with it. He was just going to have to put these issues on the back burner so that he can take care of the bigger fish.

So now he was stuck with a dilemma cause he had to tell Cheryl about the girls. Stone called her so that he can talk to her and give her the news ASAP.

"Hey baby what's up with you is everything good?"

"Yeah. But I do need to talk to you about a few things."

She did not know what he must talk to her about. Don't hold back daddy let me know what you have on your mind. She only said that cause she knows enough of him to know when he is choosing his words wisely.

"I want to talk to you about Cindy and China. China is pregnant and the streets are getting real hectic right now. The feds are watching Murder, I don't know what they know about the rest, China has to come, and Cindy wants to follow." He then paused a second and waited to see what her response was going to be.

"So, what does all that have to do with me Stone? I know those are your ride or dies, I was not born yesterday! I also want you to know that this is your kingdom and you can run it anyway you want as long as you love me and the baby."

"Of course, I will love you Cheryl don't be silly. I just know for a fact that the police are not onto me as of yet. So, home will be the safest place for them to go and lay low. I will just have to explain to them that you are going to have my child also but that will be when I bring them."

"That's your problem Stone not mine cause I am comfortable with the decision I made. I am a grow woman that understand the way the game is, and I am all game for what comes."

"You are a great woman to me Cheryl I swear. I thank you for being so understanding with me and my problems. I will be seeing you real soon I am going to pick them up right now."

"Now let me ask you Stone can you handle all that pussy in one household" Cheryl joked.

"I am not worried about keeping the three of you satisfied sexually right now. I just know I have good women around me that are the few people I trust in this world. So, if the day comes when I no longer be here and get sent back to the essence. I know all my kids and those I love would be taken care of!"

"Stop talking like that and go get Cindy and China before it gets too late. Everything is going to be fine as long as they can understand I got knocked up by you."

"I'm on my way right now to pick them up Cheryl and stop being so bossy" Stone joked. He was just happy that Cheryl was so understanding to his lifestyle and the choices he made with them.

As he was on his way to the Bronx leaving Blast house he called Sin first to make sure she was ready. For he knew she was always taking her time when it came to doing things for, she was always picky with her doings. That was his heart and to think that he had to tell her about Cheryl gave him butterflies in his stomach. What he had to tell her was very hard only cause he knew it was going to break her heart.

"What is up baby are you ready to be out? I am on my way right now so be ready to leave. You not going to need anything where you going to move too! Just make sure you bring my bag with you there is a lot of money in there. Everything a person could need will be there for you. So please let's make this trip fast for me the quicker we get out the hood the better for all of us!"

"Well in that case I am all ready to leave sweetheart. But what are we going to do with all the shit I have bought for the crib? You know I have a lot of furniture that is very expensive in my apartment. It makes me sad to leave all this good stuff behind."

"Don't worry about that somebody would buy all the furniture. I have peoples that will sell all your furniture, so you do not have to worry about taking a lost. Worst case scenario we can put it on Craigslist." He only said what she wanted to hear at the moment.

"I'm going to be honest with you Stone, I could care less of all the materialistic shit I'm leaving behind. At the end of the day I am just glad we are moving on and leaving all this behind."

"Great then I call you when I get there," He hung the phone up with her then called China. It was as if they were two of the same because she asked the same questions and felt the same way about the changes, they are doing with their lives. The only thing that he had to worry about was when he took them to his house how would the girls react when they find out that he has gotten Cheryl pregnant.

It took all day to get them on the road and leave after giving them more than enough time. Even when he gave them the heads up that he was on his way to pick them up. He told them that they did not need anything and it was still hard for them to leave it all behind and took as much as they could with them. They all sat quiet during the trip to Stone house all in their own deep thought. The girls went along with him only because the greatest memories they had come when they were with Stone. So, it did not take much persuading to move on with him. But for Stone it made him nervous to know that they were about to get to his house and his secret was ready to be out in the open concerning Loose Cheryl.

When they almost reached their destination. Stone stop the car got out and told the girls to do the same. They did not know why he stopped but whatever it was they knew it was of importance.

"Why are we stopping in the middle of the road Stone?" Sin was a bit confused for she has not seen him act like this in a long time. To be honest she never seen him nervous about anything before.

"Just get out I have to give you the breakdown on all that is going on with us." The girls followed timidly for they did not know what was going on. He explained to them about the day police trailed him to the restaurant. He let them know shit is about to get ugly and from this moment on they had to go low. That is when he told them to toss their phones and made them swear that they will never set foot in the Bronx again. "You need to understand I am only doing this to protect you."

The girls did as he said because all this time, they wanted out of the lifestyle they have been living. So, giving up the game is something that they were dying to have the opportunity to do. They hated everything about the street life except for Stone and the cash they earn. Once he got that out the way they hopped back in the car and drove to the house.

When Stone pointed the house out to the girls, they could not believe how beautiful it was. They instantly fell in love with it and where so happy that they are going to live in a house so huge.

"Now that we are home, I have something else that I have been wanting to tell you but did not know how. But since you are here now there is no way of telling you but by just being straight up."

"Come on papi you know you could tell me anything." Sin loved him to death so there is not too much he could tell her to disappoint her. Whatever it is she knows she can get pass it. She knew him so well that by the way he has been acting there was something he was dying to tell her.

"I know Sin but I just did not have the courage to do it. But since we are here you going to see for yourself, there is no holding back now." He caressed her face for even though he has two baby mamas to be it is Sin that he is in love with. She was the perfect mate a woman that has always brought out the best out of him.

"Just tell me who she is Stone." Sin knew Stone well and knew the only thing he would hold back is if he was with another female.

"Let's just go inside so that the two of you could see for yourselves. This is something that has been bothering me greatly and I hope that it does not do the same to you."

They walked into the house and the first thing that hit them was the smell in the kitchen. There was some home cooking going on. They looked amazed at the home that Stone has been holding out on them. When they walked into the kitchen everyone froze without saying a word. It was as if time has stopped so that everyone can get their thoughts in order.

Sin was glad that it was Cheryl that was living with Stone. Everything changed the moment she looked at her stomach and saw she was having a baby. She got highly upset and instantly to hate both for it. Stone did not only get China pregnant but he got Cheryl pregnant also. She dealt with so many emotions at that moment. In which took all of her to not lose her cool.

"Let me ask you Stone are you the one that got her pregnant?"

He never got to answer her questioned because Cheryl changed the subject.

"Come on girls let me show you each of your rooms and the house that is going to be your home. I knew that the two of you were on your way and I made arrangements to make it as homely to you as it is already for me."

They did not say anything but as they walked off Sin looked into Stones eyes and he saw the hatred in her eyes. He knew she was someone not to play with and hoped that she can forgive him for this one.

He was going to let it play out whichever way it did cause at the end of the day there is more serious issues that need handling. His thoughts went to the streets and all the shit that is about to go down. Now that they are out of harm's way, Stone must Strategize his next move. This move must be his best move. Since he knew that there is not a soul, he could trust to get out the game. He had to use a few to help him in his cause outside of his circle. This deep in the game to get out only means death or prison. Stone is not going to except either as an option. He was going to do the opposite and get rid of the biggest problem. This was every street dude's worse nightmare in which they can have and that is to go to war with people out of their league. For Stone it was a major player by the name of Manolo and his associates

TO THE READER

The everyday struggle truthfully speaking is inside of us. We as human beings have the power to choose the person we want to be and pursue the life we want to live. But if it's one thing that is certain hard are always around the corner. These times do not determine who we are as long as we can visualize and have the strength to overcome one's obstacle. That is why I am the first to admit that our worst enemy is seen in the reflection of the mirror!!

I have personally been to hell and back but was not able to return until I came to the realization that it is I that is making my own hell on earth. I was always quick to blame everything and everyone as conspirers to my downfall. But I never took the time to sit back and analyze what I was, THE PROBLEM! We all have qualities inside of us that are going to make the man or destroy the person. I am talking about our emotions, our thoughts, our principles, our values, and when they are not in order the monster that grows inside of us, which makes us hardened criminals, menace to society, and terrorist to our communities.

I became a part of that chaotic under world that destroyed the same communities my love ones where raised in. Many said to have loved me, but none were truly my friends. To tell me truth, that I have become insane. Each day I sank deeper into the game to the point that I lost my true identity, the person MAMA raised. I got so blinded by the money, women, and everything that the games bring that I imprisoned myself to four corners that the only outcome where death, prison, or the matrix.

Even though I can say that I am free from that chaos or the system for the time being. I have met so many lifers that are good men in general, but a few seconds of mixed emotions cause them their lives, send to the essence, labeled as murderers, treated as livestock, or just seen as inhuman. It's not fair but that is what the reality for us is today.

I speak out to all because I have experienced the lifestyle and dealt with the drama that I only put myself through. You tend to live in regret when you find out that it is only self that put one through these hard times. But I rather live in regret and have the chance to get my life in order. Then blame the world blocking out the reality that I am committing suicide slowly.

—MR. GRAMM

CPSIA information can be obtained
at www.ICGtesting.com
Printed in the USA
FSHW011534031019
62653FS